Catherine Spencer

THE ITALIAN'S CONVENIENT WIFE

ITALIAN HUSBANDS

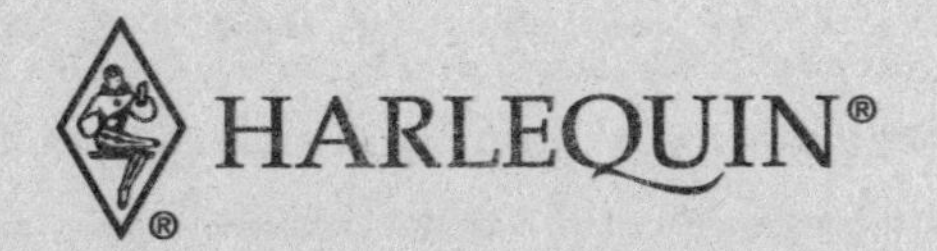

TORONTO • NEW YORK • LONDON
AMSTERDAM • PARIS • SYDNEY • HAMBURG
STOCKHOLM • ATHENS • TOKYO • MILAN • MADRID
PRAGUE • WARSAW • BUDAPEST • AUCKLAND

ISBN-13: 978-0-373-12552-4
ISBN-10: 0-373-12552-6

THE ITALIAN'S CONVENIENT WIFE

First North American Publication 2006.

This edition published by arrangement with Harlequin Books S.A.

www.eHarlequin.com

Printed in U.S.A.

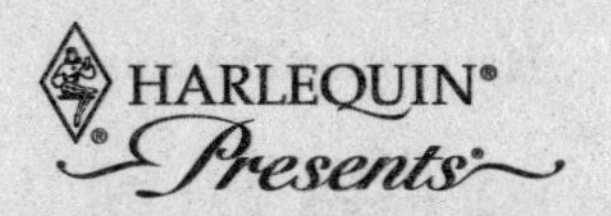

Great news! From this month onward, Harlequin Presents® is offering you more!

Now, when you go to your local bookstore, you'll find that you have *eight* Harlequin Presents® titles to choose from—more of your favorite authors, more of the stories you love.

To help you make your selection from our July books, here are the fabulous titles that are available: *Prince of the Desert* by Penny Jordan—hot desert nights! *The Scorsolini Marriage Bargain* by Lucy Monroe—the final part of an unforgettable royal trilogy! *Naked in His Arms* by Sandra Marton—the third Knight Brothers story and a sensationally sensual read to boot! *The Secret Baby Revenge* by Emma Darcy—a passionate Latin lover and a shocking secret from his past! *At the Greek Tycoon's Bidding* by Cathy Williams—an ordinary girl and the most gorgeous Greek millionaire! *The Italian's Convenient Wife* by Catherine Spencer—passion, tears and joy as a marriage is announced! *The Jet-Set Seduction* by Sandra Field—fasten your seat belt and prepare to be whisked away to glamorous foreign locations! *Mistress on Demand* by Maggie Cox—he's rich, ruthless and really...irresistible!

Remember, in July, Harlequin Presents® promises more reading pleasure. Enjoy!

All about the author...
Catherine Spencer

Some people know practically from birth that they're going to be writers. CATHERINE wasn't one of them. Her first idea was to be a nun, which was clearly never going to work! A series of other choices followed. She considered becoming a veterinarian (but she lacked the emotional stamina to deal with sick and injured animals), a hairdresser (until she overheated a curling iron and singed the hair off the top of her best friend's head the day before her first date), a nurse (but that meant emptying bedpans!). As a last resort, she became a high school English teacher, and loved it.

Eventually, she married, had four children and, always, always, a dog or two or three. How can a house become a home without a dog? In time, the children grew up and moved out on their own and she returned to teaching, but a middle-aged restlessness overtook her and she looked for a change of career.

What's an English teacher's area of expertise? Well, novels, among other things, and moody, brooding, unforgettable heroes: Heathcliff, Edward Fairfax Rochester, Romeo and Rhett Butler. Then there's that picky business of knowing how to punctuate and spell, and all those rules of grammar. They all pointed her in the same direction: breaking the rules every chance she got, and creating her own moody, brooding unforgettable heroes. And that's where she happily resides now, in Harlequin Presents, of course.

CHAPTER ONE

CALLIE had been eighteen the last time that deep, dark Mediterranean voice had seduced her into forgetting everything her mother had taught her about "saving" herself for the "right" man. The kind who'd greet her at the altar with a full appreciation for what her pristine white gown and flowing veil signified. The kind who'd cherish the prized gift of her virginity on their wedding night.

Eighteen.

Nine years and a lifetime ago.

Yet although the phone awoke her from a deep sleep at the ungodly hour of four in the morning, she recognized at once who was calling. And so did her heart. It contracted as painfully as if a huge fist had closed around it and was squeezing the very life from her body.

"It is Paolo Rainero, Caroline," he said. And then, as if she needed further clarification, "Ermanno's brother. Your sister's brother-in-law."

And my first love. My first lover. The only one.

Callie cleared her throat. Swallowed. *"Buon giorno,"* she said, groping for the bedside lamp, and wished her Italian rolled off her tongue with the same fluid, exotic ease that he brought to English. "What a surprise to hear from you after all this time, Paolo. How are you?"

He let a beat of time pass before answering, and in that short but endless silence, any fledgling hope she'd entertained that he was in the U.S., and wanted to renew acquaintance with her for the pure pleasure of her company, shriveled and died. Fear slithered up her spine, leaving her skin unpleasantly clammy, and she knew with sudden, chilling certainty that he had nothing good to tell her.

As if to ward off the blow he was about to deliver, she asked with desperate good cheer, "Where are you calling from?"

"Rome. Caroline—"

"Are you sure? You sound as close as if you're just next door. I'd never have guessed you're half a world away. It's amazing what—"

He recognized her mindless babble for the delaying tactic it was. "Caroline," he said again, cutting her off more forcefully this time, "I'm afraid I have bad news."

The children! Something had happened to the children!

Her mouth ran dry. Freed from the vicious hold, her heart hurled itself into a punishing, uneven beat somewhere in the vicinity of her stomach. "How bad?" she asked shakily.

"Very bad, *cara.* There has been a yachting accident. An explosion at sea." He paused again. Another horribly telling hesitation. "Ermanno and Vanessa were aboard at the time."

"With the children?" She forced the question past parched lips.

"No. With four guests and a crew of six. They left the children with my parents."

A thread of relief wound its way through her mounting dread. "And? Don't leave me hanging like this, Paolo. How badly is my sister hurt?"

"I'm saddened to have to tell you, there were no survivors."

The softly lit room swam before her eyes. "None at all?"

"None."

Her beautiful, generous, loving sister dead? Her body blown to pieces, mutilated beyond recognition?

Callie scrunched her eyes shut against the horrifying images filling her mind. Clutching the phone in a white-knuckled grip, she whispered, "How can you be so sure?"

"The explosion was visible for miles. Other yachts in the area raced to the scene to lend assistance. Search and rescue vessels went into immediate operation. Their efforts met with no success. It was clear no one could have survived such a blast."

"But what if they were thrown into the sea and made it to shore? What if you stopped searching too soon? Vanessa's a strong swimmer. She might—"

"No, Caroline," he said. "It is not possible. The devastation was too great, the evidence, too…graphic to be mistaken for anything other than what it was."

He had never before spoken to her with such kindness; with such compassion. That he did so now nearly killed her.

A huge balloon of grief rose in her throat, almost choking her. A sound filled her ears; echoed repeatedly in the dimly lit bedroom. A sound so primitive, she could barely conceive that it poured from her.

Paolo's voice pierced the black, terrible mists enveloping her. "Is there anyone with you, Caroline?"

What sort of question was that? And by what right did he, of all people, dare to ask it? "It's not yet dawn, and I'm in bed," she said rawly. "Alone."

His voice caressed her. "You should not be, not at a time like this."

Not in bed? she wondered. *Or not alone?*

"You are in shock, as are we all," he continued, clarifying his remark. "Is there no one you can call on, to help you get through the next few hours until the necessary travel arrangements are in place?"

"Travel?"

"To Rome. For the funerals. They will take place later in the week. Naturally you will attend."

Naturally! Nonetheless, she bristled at his tone, so clearly that of a man not accustomed to being thwarted. Some things never changed.

"I'll be there," she said. "How are the children coping?"

"Not well. They're old enough to understand what death means. They know they'll never again see their parents. Gina cries often, and although he tries to be brave, I know that Clemente sheds many a private tear, too."

Pushing aside her own grief to make room for theirs, Callie said, "Please give them my love and tell them their…their aunt Callie will see them soon."

"Of course—for what it's worth."

Anger knifed through her, intense as forked lightning. "Are you questioning my sincerity, Paolo?"

"Not in the least," he replied smoothly. "I'm simply stating a fact. Of course the twins are aware they have an aunt who lives in America, but they don't *know* you. You're a name, a photograph, someone who never forgets to send them lovely gifts at Christmas and on their birthdays, or postcards from the interesting foreign places you visit. But you found the time to come to see them only once, when they were infants and much too young to remember you. For the rest, you depended on their parents to bring them to America to visit you—and how often did that occur? Two, three times, in the last eight years?"

His sigh drifted gently, regretfully, over the phone. "The unfortunate truth is, Caroline, you and the children are almost strangers to one other. A sad case of 'out of sight, out of mind,' I'm afraid."

He might see it that way, but Callie knew differently. Not a day went by that she didn't think of those two adorable children. She spent hours poring over fat albums of photographs depicting every stage in their lives, from when they were just a few hours old, to the present day. Her staircase wall was filled with framed pictures of them. Their most recent portraits occupied pride of place by her bed, on the mantelpiece in her living room, on her desk at the office. She could have picked them out unerringly in a crowd of hundreds of children with the same dark hair and brown eyes, so well did she know every feature, every expression, every tiny detail that made them unique.

Strangers, Paolo? In your dreams!

"Nonetheless, I *am* their aunt, and they can count on me to be there for them now," she told him. "I'll leave here tomorrow and barring any unforeseen delays, should be with them the day after that."

"Then I'll send you the details of your flight later today."

"Please don't trouble yourself, Paolo," she said coolly. "I can well afford to make my own reservations, and will take care of them myself."

"No, Caroline, you will not," he said flatly. "This has nothing to do with money, it has to do with family looking after family—and regardless of how *you* might perceive it, we are inextricably connected through the marriage of your sister to my brother, are we not?"

Oh, yes, Paolo, she thought, smothering the burst of hysterical laughter rising in her throat at the irony of his question. *That, and a whole lot more than you can begin to imagine!*

Mistaking her silence for disagreement, he said, "This is no time to quibble over the fine print of our association, Caroline. No matter which way you look at it, we have a niece and nephew in common, and must rally together for their good."

How nauseatingly self-righteous he sounded! How morally upright! If she hadn't known better, Callie might have been fooled into believing he really was as honorable and responsible as he made himself out to be.

"I couldn't agree more, Paolo," she said, with deceptive meekness. "I wouldn't dream of turning my back on the twins when they need all the emotional support they can get. I'll be in Rome no later than Tuesday."

"And you will allow me to make your flight arrangements?"

Why not? Pride had no place in the tragic loss of her sister, and Callie was having trouble enough holding herself together. She couldn't afford to squander her strength when she had much bigger battles to wage than besting Paolo Rainero on the trifling matter of who sprang for the price of her ticket. She could pay him back later, when everything else was settled. "If you insist."

"*Eccellente!* Thank you for seeing things my way."

You won't thank me for long, Paolo, she thought. *Not once you discover that when I come home again, I'm bringing those children with me!*

Outside the converted eighteenth-century palazzo whose entire top floor housed his parents' apartment, the traffic and crowds, both so much a part of everyday Rome, went about their noisy business as usual. Immediately beyond the leather-paneled walls of his father's library, however, a mournful hush reigned. Dropping the receiver back in its cradle, Paolo left the room and made his way down the long hall to the day salon where his parents waited.

His mother had aged ten years in the last two days. Weeping and sleeplessness left her beautiful eyes ringed with shadows. Her mouth trembled uncontrollably. Silver, which surely hadn't been there a week ago, glinted in her thick black hair. She clutched his father's hand almost convulsively, as if only by doing so could she anchor herself to sanity.

"Well? How did she take the news? Is she coming for the

funerals?" Cultured, wealthy in his own right, influential, and deeply respected in the international world of high finance, Salvatore Rainero did not surrender easily to defeat. But Paolo heard it in the subdued tone with which his father uttered the questions; recognized it in the slump of those broad, patrician shoulders.

"She'll be here." Paolo shrugged wearily, his own sense of loss lying heavy in the pit of his stomach. "As for how she took the news, she was shocked, bereft, as are we all."

His mother dabbed at her eyes with a fine linen handkerchief. "Did she mention the children?"

"Yes, but nothing that you need to worry about. She sent them her love."

"Does she have any idea that—?"

"None. Nor did it occur to her to ask. But she was unprepared for my call and most probably not thinking clearly. It's possible she might wonder, over the next two days. And even if she does not, once they're read, we won't be able to hide the terms of the wills from her."

His mother let out an anguished moan. "And who's to say how she will react?"

"She may react any way she pleases, Lidia," Paolo's father said grimly, "but she will not create havoc with our grandchildren, because I will not allow her to do so. In declining to take an active role in their lives for the past eight years, she forfeits the right to have any say in their future." His fierce gaze swung to Paolo. "Did you have to work hard to persuade her to let us bring her over here at our expense?"

"Not particularly."

"Good!" A spark of triumph lightened the grief in the old man's eyes. "Then she can be bought."

"Oh, Salvatore, that's cruel!" his wife objected. "Caroline is mourning her sister's death too deeply to care about monetary matters."

"I have to agree," Paolo felt obliged to add. "I suspect the poor thing was so numbed by my news that I could have persuaded her the moon was made of cheese, if I'd put my mind to it. Once she gets past the initial shock of this tragedy, she might well change her mind about accepting our offer. We met only briefly and nine years ago at that, but I remember her as being a singularly proud and independent young woman."

"You're wrong, both of you." His father heaved himself up from the sofa to pace the length of the room. "She was anything but proud in the way she threw herself at you after the wedding, Paolo. If you'd given her the slightest encouragement, you'd soon have followed in your brother's footsteps, and found yourself at the altar, too."

Again, Paolo's mother spoke up, unnaturally vigorous in her defense of someone she hardly knew, he thought. "You're being unfair, Salvatore! I spoke to Caroline at length when she was here, and she was very excited about starting her university studies that September. I don't believe she'd have abandoned her plans, even if Paolo *had* encouraged her."

But there was no *even if* about it, Paolo thought, a disconcerting pang of shame rising from the ashes of the murky memories suddenly looming up in his mind. Despite his many other excesses in those days, alcohol wasn't among them. But the night of his brother's wedding, he'd had too much champagne to remember much beyond the fact that the bride's pretty sister had been young, impressionable, eminently desirable and willing—though not nearly as experienced as she'd pretended to be.

One night with a novice had been enough to make him regret having seduced her. He wasn't accustomed to his women being so generous, so trustingly naive. Caroline's wide-eyed innocence, her sincerity and simple *goodness,* unnerved him—*him,* Paolo Giovanni Vittorio Rainero, a man afraid of nothing and no one. But she'd made him look too deep inside himself and he hadn't liked what he saw.

He was the one who came from a long line of blue bloods, yet beside her he felt undeserving; an emotional pauper with little of worth to offer a girl who could have been a princess. She deserved better than what he could give her.

Facing her the next morning…well, in all truth, he hadn't. Couldn't. Her lowered gaze, the crushed disappointment touching her lovely mouth, and knowing he was the one who had put them there, had been more than he could bear. Hangover notwithstanding, he'd made a fast escape.

He hadn't expected to run into her again, when he stopped by his parents' apartment, a few days after the wedding. But he'd recognized at once that her earlier infatuation for him had metamorphosed into chilly disgust. A week had been more than long enough for her to realize Paolo Rainero wasn't at all her kind of man.

Judging from the tone of their recent phone call, time hadn't exactly mellowed her opinion of him. If his parents' hopes for the future were to be realized, he was going to have to work very hard to polish his image, and charm her into compliance by whatever means necessary.

The realization did not sit well with him. In fact, it left a distinctly bad taste in his mouth. Seduction for seduction's sake, whether or not it involved the physical, had long since lost its flavor, especially when it came with a hidden agenda.

"Where are the twins now?" he inquired.

"Tullia took them to the park," his father said. "We thought a change of scene would be good for them."

Paolo thought so, too. Huge bouquets had arrived daily since the accident, tokens of sympathy from the family's vast circle of friends and acquaintances. The overpowering scent of lilies filled the apartment with funereal solemnity. There'd be enough of that at the church on Saturday, and again on Monday, when the immediate family accompanied the remains to the island for the private burial rites.

His mother drifted to the balcony overlooking the rear courtyard. "I don't know how the children would cope without Tullia," she said fretfully. "She's been with them since they were babies, and they cling to her now. They seem to need her more than they need us."

"And they need us more than they need an aunt they wouldn't know from Adam," Salvatore interjected, slipping an arm around her waist and leading her from the room. "Come, Lidia, my love. Stop worrying about Caroline Leighton and start looking after yourself. You've barely closed your eyes since we heard the dreadful news, and you need to rest."

She went unresistingly, but turned in the doorway at the last second. "Will you still be here later, Paolo?"

"Yes," he said, his glance locking briefly with his father's and correctly reading the plea he saw there. "I'll be here for as long as you both need me. You can count on me to do whatever must be done to keep our family intact."

Although determined to keep such a promise, he hoped he could do so and not end up despising himself for the methods he might have to employ.

The Air France Boeing 777-200 touched down at Charles de Gaulle airport in Paris just after eleven o'clock on the Tuesday morning, completing the first leg of her journey to Rome. She'd left San Francisco exactly ten hours earlier, which wasn't such an inordinately long time to be in the air, especially not when she'd reclined in Executive Class comfort the entire distance. But the fact that it was only two in the morning, Pacific Standard Time, played havoc with Callie's inner clock, not to mention her appearance.

She'd never been able to cry prettily, the way some women could, and her face bore unmistakable evidence of weeping. It would take considerable cosmetic expertise and every spare second of the two hours before her connecting flight to Rome, to disguise the ravages of grief. But disguise them she would, because when she faced Paolo Rainero again, she intended to be in control—of herself and the situation.

Perhaps if, after deplaning, she'd been less involved in plotting her strategies, she might have noticed him sooner. As it was, she'd have walked straight past him if he hadn't planted himself so firmly in her path that she almost tripped over his feet.

"*Ciao,* Caroline," he greeted her, and before she had time to recover from the impact of Paolo Rainero's voice assaulting her yet again out of the blue, he'd caught her by the shoulders and bent his head to press a light, continental kiss on each of her cheeks.

She'd wondered if she'd recognize him. If he'd changed much in nine years. If the dissolute life he'd pursued in his early twenties had left only the crumbling remains of his formerly stunning good looks. Would the aristocratic planes of his face have disappeared under a sagging layer of flesh, with his sleek olive skin crisscrossed by a road map of broken veins? Would his middle have grown soft, his hairline receded?

She'd prayed it would be so. It would make seeing him again so much easier. But the man confronting her had lost nothing of his masculine beauty. Rather, he had redefined it.

His shoulders had broadened with maturity, his chest deepened, but not an ounce of fat clung to his frame. The clean, hard line of his jaw, the firm contours of his mouth, spoke of single-minded purpose. There was dignity and strength in his bearing. Authority in his somber, dark brown gaze.

He had a full head of hair. Thick, black, silky hair that begged a woman to run her fingers through it. And only the faintest trace of laugh lines fanned out from the corners of his eyes.

Stunned, she stared at him, all hope that he'd prove himself as susceptible to the passage of time as any other man, evaporating in a rush of molten awareness that battered her with the force of a tornado.

It wasn't fair. He'd shown a flagrant disregard for the frailty of human life, driving too fast, living on the edge, and daring death to slow him down. At the very least, he might have had the good grace to look a little worn around the edges. Instead he stood there, splendidly tall and confident—and still dangerously attractive, despite the tragic reason for his coming into her life again.

Woefully conscious of her own disarray, both physical and mental, and unable to do anything about either, she stammered, "Why are you here?"

He smiled just enough for her to see that he still had all his teeth, too, and that they were every bit as white and even as she remembered. Amazing, really. She'd have thought some irate husband would have knocked a few of them out by now. Paolo had had quite a taste for other men's wives, when he wasn't seducing virgins.

"Why else would I be here, but to meet you, Caroline?"

She wanted to smack him for the way he seemed to suck the oxygen out of the atmosphere and leave her fighting to breathe. "Well, in case you've forgotten, you booked me all the way through to Rome, and we're not even in Italy yet."

"There's been a slight change of itinerary," he said, rolling his R's in melodic cadence. "You will be traveling the rest of the way with me, in the Rainero corporate jet."

"Why?"

He lifted his impeccably clad shoulders in a shrug. "Why not?"

"Because there's no need. I have a ticket on a regular flight. All other considerations apart, what about my luggage? The inconvenience of my not showing up—"

"Do not concern yourself, Caroline," he purred. "I have seen to it. By standing here throwing up obstacles, you inconvenience no one but me."

Another thing about him remained unchanged. He was as

arrogant as ever, and it was still all about him! "Well, heaven forbid you should be put out in any way, Paolo!"

He regarded her with benign tolerance, the way *she* might have regarded a fractious two-year-old trying to bite her ankle. "You are exhausted and sad, *cara,* and it's making you a little *capricciosa,*" he decided, relieving her of her carry-on bag with one hand, and cupping her elbow with the other.

"That shouldn't come as any surprise, all things considered!"

"Nor does it, which is why I thought to spare you the tedium of spending time waiting here in a crowded airport, when it is within my power to have you already safely arrived in Rome before your originally scheduled flight leaves Paris."

"I don't mind the wait." She tried ineffectually to squirm free of his hold. "I'm actually looking forward to the chance to freshen up after being cooped up in an aircraft for ten hours."

"Be assured, the company jet has excellent facilities, all of which are at your disposal," he countered. "Come, now, Caroline. Allow me to spoil you a little, especially now when you have all you can do to hold yourself together."

Supremely confident that he'd overcome her objections, he swept her out of the terminal and into the back of a waiting limousine. After a brief exchange with the uniformed driver, Paolo joined her, settling himself beside her close enough that his body warmth crept out to touch her.

Unnerved, she inched farther into the corner as the car joined the traffic heading out of the airport toward the city center. Noticing, he smiled and said, "Try to relax, *cara.* I am not abducting you and I intend you no harm. You're perfectly safe with me."

Safe with him? Not if he was anything like the man he'd been nine years ago! Yet his concern seemed genuine. He appeared more tuned in to her feelings, and less focused on his own. Could she have misjudged him, and he had changed, after all?

Callie supposed anything was possible. Heaven knew, *she* was nothing like the girl he'd seduced, then cast aside so callously. Perhaps they'd both grown up.

"Ah!" His shoulder brushed hers as he leaned past her to look out of the window. "We'll soon be there."

Huddling even farther into the corner, she said, "Where's 'there' exactly?"

"Le Bourget. It's the airport most commonly used by private jets."

Soon—much too soon for Callie's peace of mind—they arrived, and in short order had cleared security, passed through the departure gate and were crossing the open tarmac to where a Lear jet waited, its engines idling. Buffeted by the wind, she mounted the steps to the interior, and barely had time to fasten her seat belt before the aircraft was cleared for takeoff.

Was she crazy to have allowed Paolo to coerce her into changing her travel plans? she wondered, as Paris fell away below, and the jet turned its nose to the southeast. Did he have an ulterior motive? Or was she looking for trouble where none existed?

"You're very silent, Caroline," he observed, some half hour later. "Very withdrawn."

"I just lost my sister," she said. "I'm not exactly in a party mood."

"Nor am I suggesting you should be, but it occurs to me you might wish to discuss the funeral arrangements…." He paused fractionally, his long fingers idly caressing a glass of sparkling water. "Or the children."

"No," she said, turning to stare at the great expanse of blue sky beyond the porthole to her left. "Not right now. It's all I can do to come to terms with the fact that I'll never see Vanessa again. I keep hoping to wake up and find it's all a horrible dream. Perhaps once I've seen the children, and your parents…. How are *they* coping with this terrible tragedy, by the way? Your parents, I mean?"

"They're even more devastated than you claim to be."

Sure she must not have heard him correctly, she swung back to face him and found him watching her with chilling intensity. "Are you suggesting I'm *faking* how I feel, Paolo?"

Raising his glass, he rotated it so that its cut crystal facets caught the light and flung it at her in a blur of dazzling reflections. "Well, if you are," he said silkily, "it wouldn't be the first time, would it, *cara?*"

There was nothing kindly in his regard now, nothing compassionate, nor did he pretend otherwise. In that instant, she knew that she should have listened to her instincts. Because, in stepping aboard the Rainero corporate jet, she'd made a fatal mistake.

She'd put herself at the mercy of a man who, whatever his stated reasons for meeting her in Paris, no more cared about her now than he had nine years ago. He was exactly the same callous heel who had ruined her life once, and given half a chance, he'd do the very same thing a second time.

CHAPTER TWO

"SO YOU don't bother to lash out at me for such a remark?" he drawled. "You don't take exception to the fact that I imply you're less than honest?"

Swamped in an anger directed as much at herself as at him, Callie retorted, "Don't mistake my silence for an admission of guilt, Paolo. It's simply that I'm floored by your audacity. You may rest assured I take *very* great exception to your accusation."

"But you don't deny the truth of it?"

"Of course I do!" she spat. "I have *never* lied to you."

"Never? Not even by omission?"

Again, she was left speechless, but from fear, this time. He couldn't know the truth—not unless Vanessa or Ermanno had told him.

Oh, surely not! They stood to gain nothing by doing so, and would have lost what they most cared about.

"You've turned rather pale, Caroline." Utterly remorseless, Paolo continued to torment her. "Could it be that you remember, after all?"

Less certain of herself by the second, Callie fought to match his offhand manner. "Remember what, exactly?"

"The day your sister married my brother—or more precisely, the night following the wedding."

So her secret was safe, after all! But as relief washed over her, so, too, did a wave of embarrassment. "Oh," she muttered, helpless to stem the heat flooding her face. *"That!"*

"*That,* indeed. Let me see if I recall events accurately." Ever so casually, he tapped the rim of his water glass. "There was a moon, and many, many stars. A beach with powder-soft sand, lapped by lazy, lukewarm waves. A cabana that offered privacy. You in a dress that begged to be removed…and I—"

"All right," Callie snapped. "You've made your point. I remember."

As if she could forget—and heaven knew she'd tried hard enough to do just that! It was the night she gave him her virginity, her innocence and her heart. Not even the slow passage of nine years could dim the clarity of those memories….

"Isn't he the most divinely handsome man you've ever seen?" Radiant in her pearl and crystal encrusted wedding gown, Vanessa had peeked from behind the drapes fluttering at the French windows of the suite set aside for the bride and her attendants. In the grounds below, her groom chatted with the more than three hundred guests who'd arrived that morning in a flotilla of private yachts, and were now milling about the terrace.

As weddings went, Callie supposed this one came as close to fairy-tale perfection as reality could get. *Isola di Gemma,* the Raineros's private island, was aptly named—truly a jewel, set in the shimmering Adriatic, some thirty miles off the coast of Italy.

But, like her sister, she barely noticed the huge urns of exotic blooms framing the flower-draped arch where the ceremony was to take place, or the rows of elegant white wrought-iron chairs linked together with white satin streamers. Instead she inched out onto the narrow Juliet balcony, the better to spy on the groom's tall, dark-haired younger brother, busy adjusting the gardenia in the lapel of his white jacket.

He'd landed by helicopter on the island the night before, arriving just in time for dinner, and Callie's mouth had run dry at the sight of him. Charming and handsome, with a worldly sophistication to match his good looks, he reduced the young men she usually dated to pitifully clumsy boys.

She hadn't been able to stop thinking about him since. She'd even dreamed about him. Vanessa's wedding might be a fairly tale, but in Callie's opinion, the best man was the stuff princes were made of.

"Yes," she breathed to her sister, leaning over the balcony to get a better view. "He's...divine."

Perfect. God-like!

As if he could read her mind, he glanced up, trained his gaze directly on her, and sent her a slow, conspiratorial smile, as if, between them, they harbored a secret too deliciously wicked to be shared with anyone else. At that, an unfamiliar sensation trickled through her, startling and sweet. Suddenly weak at the knees, she clutched the balcony railing.

"Come away from there, both of you," their mother had scolded. "It's bad luck for the groom to see the bride beforehand, and while having the maid of honor fall headlong from an upper floor balcony might amuse some people, I doubt it would impress your future father-in-law, Vanessa."

How true! Salvatore Rainero had made scant secret of the fact that he had reservations about his son's marriage to an American. That he considered Audrey Leighton and her two daughters socially inferior, and quite possibly fortune hunters, had been apparent from the outset, but Ermanno had remained adamant. He intended to marry Vanessa with, or without, his father's approval.

Fortunately his mother, Lidia, had scoffed at her husband's suspicions, and given the couple her blessing, thus smoothing over the tensions threatening their future. Whatever his other personality flaws, Salvatore was a doting husband who adored his wife. If she was willing to embrace into the family their son's choice of a mate, he'd swallow his misgivings and indulge her wish to throw a lavish wedding.

And lavish it was, with champagne enough to float a boat, a feast worthy of royalty—the Raineros actually had been members of the nobility in times gone by, which probably accounted for Salvatore's elevated notions of grandeur—and a two-foot high wedding cake created by an army of Rome's most renowned bakers and pastry chefs. For Callie, though, the high point of the whole affair had been when the best man escorted her onto the dance floor and took her in his arms.

She melted in the warmth of his dark-eyed gaze, in the bold intimacy of his hands sliding down her spine and urging her close. Intoxicated by his scent, by the sheer power of his masculine aura, she let him mold her body to his, and cared not one iota that his father scowled from the sidelines.

"So beautiful *una damigella d'onore* outshines the bride," Paolo murmured hotly in her ear. "It is my good fortune that my brother chose to marry your sister, and left me with the greater prize."

No boyfriend had ever spoken to her with such unfettered, lyrical passion, nor held her so close that she could feel the hard thrust of his arousal pressing against her, undeterred by a pair of finely tailored black trousers or the folds of a silk chiffon bridesmaid's gown.

No boyfriend had dared slide his arm so far around her waist that he could brush his fingers up the under-slope of her breast and, in so doing, incite a wash of heat between her legs.

All of which, she concluded dizzily, was what separated the man from the boys.

Later, he danced with his mother, the mother of the bride, and the other four bridesmaids. Waltzed sedately with an elderly widowed aunt. Twirled the flower girls around the terrace, much to their shrieking delight. Boogied with other men's wives, then returned them to their husbands, flushed and breathless and decidedly reluctant to let him go.

Finally, with the wedding festivities reaching a fever pitch of laughter and music and wine, he sought out Callie again.

"Come with me, *la mia bella,*" he urged, tugging her by the hand beyond the flare of twinkling lights illuminating the terrace, and into the shadows of the garden. "Let me show you our island, made all the more lovely by moonlight."

The mere idea left her quivering with anticipation, but, "I think we're supposed to stay until the bride and groom leave," she replied primly.

"But they will not leave," he assured her, snagging an open bottle of champagne chilling in a silver wine bucket. "Italian weddings do not end with the setting sun, *cara mia.* They are celebrated well into the small hours of the morning. We will return before anyone has the chance to miss us."

She fought a brief, losing battle with her conscience, knowing her mother wouldn't approve of her abandoning her maid-of-honor duties to run off with the best man. But wedding decorum couldn't hold a candle to Paolo's magnetic pull.

Fingers entwined with his, she followed him as he skirted the shrubbery separating the garden proper from the shore. The moon cast a path of hammered silver over the sea, and feathered in black the clumps of grass lining the beach.

"It's breathtaking," she whispered, entranced by the sight.

But Paolo grinned, his teeth blindingly white against the night-dark olive of his skin, and dragging her farther away from the light and music of the wedding, said, "You have seen nothing, yet, *bella.* Follow me."

She knew the first thread of uneasiness, then. What, after all, did she really know about him? But as if he sensed her sudden qualms, he cupped her chin and, raising her face to his, said thickly, "What, Caroline? Are you not at all the woman I took you for, but a shy, untutored girl, unused to the attentions of a man like myself? If so, you have but to speak out, and I will take you back to your *madre.*"

"No," she said, the faintly scornful laughter in his voice spurring her to recklessness. "I want to be with you, Paolo."

He kissed her then, a hot, openmouthed kiss drenched in passion. She'd never been kissed like that before, with such ardent finesse. Never savored the heated taste of a man. Never realized that the thrust and retreat of his tongue in the dark moist confines of her mouth could arouse an elemental craving for the same invasion, there in that cloistered, feminine part of her no boy had ever stirred to awareness.

Conscious of the dull, sweet ache in her lower body, she let him guide her around a small outcropping of rock, to a secluded crescent of beach. A cabana stood in the lee of the low cliff. A private, safe place, perfect for an illicit tryst.

Without a word, she went inside with him. Let him pull her down beside him on a long, cushioned bench. Laughed, and pretended she was used to champagne, drinking it directly from the bottle, as he did.

It coursed through her blood. Stripped away her inhibitions. She felt his hands toying with the tiny straps holding up her gown, the cool play of night air on her bare breasts.

In some misty recess of her mind, it occurred to her that she should stop him. But he was flicking his tongue in her ear, whispering, in Italian, words of love no sane woman could resist: *tesoro...bella...te amo...*

Then his mouth was at her breast, and she was clutching handfuls of his hair and gasping with startled pleasure. She wanted more, and so did he. She heard his muttered curse, and the whisper of fragile chiffon splitting.

He pressed her down on the bench, ran his palm under her skirt. Up her legs. Between her thighs.

She stiffened, not so much afraid, as embarrassed. She

didn't want him to discover that her satin panties were damp…there, in that private place.

He stilled his hand immediately, and lifted his head to look at her. Although moonlight filtered through the latticed window openings, his face was shadowed, preventing her from reading his expression clearly, but she heard again the sudden doubt in his voice. "You want me to stop, *cara mia?* You are, perhaps, not as eager or willing as you led me to believe?"

"Of course I am!" she whispered, at once desperate and terrified. Desperate for him to continue, and terrified that he would.

"You are sure?"

"Yes, I'm sure!" she cried, as if, by protesting loudly enough, she could silence the voice of conscience battling to be heard, and listen only to the yearning in her heart. "I want you to make love to me, Paolo."

When he seemed still to remain unconvinced, she took a hefty swallow of the champagne. Then, riding high on the false courage it gave her, she put the bottle aside and did the unthinkable. She clamped her thighs together, imprisoning his cupped hand against her. At the same time, she reached down and dared to touch him.

He was so hard and big that the fabric of his trousers was pulled taut. Enthralled, she shaped her fingers delicately over the contours of his erection.

Confined though it was by his clothing, his flesh throbbed. She could feel it. And all because of her!

His muffled groan of pleasure filled her with a heady sense of female power. All sleek muscle and tensile strength, he stood well over six feet tall. In physical confrontation with any other man, he would doubtless prove a formidable opponent. Yet she, at only five feet six inches, and weighing no more than a hundred and fifteen pounds, held him captive in the palm of her hand, both literally and figuratively. He was her prisoner; her slave!

Bolder by the second, she unsnapped the fastening of his trousers and inched open his fly. Wove her fingers inside his briefs until, freed at last, he sprang, hot and heavy and smooth as silk, into her hand.

She cradled him. Stared in dazed wonder. She wasn't entirely ignorant. She knew how men were put together. In the privacy of their rooms at the exclusive all-girls' boarding school she'd attended, she and her friends had pored over forbidden magazines and giggled furtively at illustrations that left little to the imagination. But nothing she'd learned had prepared her for the power and primitive beauty confronting her now.

"Oh!" she breathed, drawing tiny circles along his length until she reached its tip.

Any notion that she was in control fled then. With a low growl, he sent her skirt floating up around her waist, yanked off her panties and flung them carelessly to the floor. Looming over her, he pushed her legs apart and drove inside her.

Pain, sharp as slivered glass, pierced her champagne-induced euphoria, and she bit his shoulder to silence her cry. This wasn't how it was supposed to be. It should be slow and lovely and tender. He should be holding her close and telling her he loved her, not pulling away with a shocked, "*Dio!* You are *vergine?*"

Vergine—virgin!

Fiercely she locked her arms around his neck and tugged him down until her breasts lay flattened by his chest. "No," she whispered. "Don't worry, Paolo. I'm not a virgin." And it wasn't a lie, not really, even if it would have been, if she'd said the words a few minutes earlier.

"But yes!" Supporting his weight on his elbows, he stroked her cheek with trembling fingers. His voice was ragged with regret, his touch gentle. "*Tesoro,* I would not have treated you so…would not have brought you here—"

"Hush!" she protested softly, and when he went to withdraw, held his sleek, pulsing flesh captive between her thighs. Because, surprisingly, the discomfort had passed and so had the fear. Now, her body welcomed his invasion. Craved it, even. "This is what I want, it's what I need…please, Paolo!"

He remained unconvinced, however, and afraid her introduction to intimacy would end before it had properly begun, she relied on blind instinct to guide her, tilting her hips and rocking against him in flagrant invitation.

His response was immediate and powerful. Seeming driven by demons he couldn't control, he gave a moan of despair and drove deeply inside her, again and again, as if trying to outrun the enormity of something he wished he'd never started but hadn't a hope of stopping.

Finding herself again in unknown territory, Callie tried to respond appropriately to the wild ride she'd initiated. She wasn't sure what was expected of her, or how it would end, but she was very sure that she didn't want to disappoint him.

She found, though, that it wasn't so difficult to match her rhythm to his, or to murmur his name with heartfelt desire. When the tempo of their lovemaking increased, her little cry of pleasure was unpremeditated. When she dug her nails into his shoulders, she did so with unrehearsed joy and a real sense of anticipation.

Then he spoke, his words urgent with command. "*Si,*" he panted, cupping her bottom and seeming to hold himself on the brink of destruction. "Don't hold back, *tesoro!* Let it happen now! Let me feel you come!"

And at that, she froze.

Come? She didn't have a clue how to come! But she knew she was supposed to, and she knew if she didn't that she'd disappoint him after all, and she'd seen enough movies to have some idea of what orgasm was all about, and what did one more little deception matter at this stage of the game? So she thrashed her head from side to side, jiggled convulsively up and down on the bench, and uttered a long-drawn-out, breathy, *When Harry Met Sally* kind of "Ooh! Ooh, Paolo, *yes!*"

It seemed to work because, after a brief, disbelieving pause, Paolo tensed, shuddered violently, then collapsed on top of her, his chest heaving.

It was over. She'd survived her ordeal by fire and emerged relatively unscathed—or so she believed until he pulled away from her, and drawled, "We'll take a rest, then try that again, Caroline. And the next time, you *will* come."

She wished the earth would open up and swallow her. But by then too deep into a charade entirely of her own making to escape, she continued the lie. "I don't know what you mean, Paolo."

"No," he said, disgust and amusement layering his voice. "I'm well aware of that. But it will be my pleasure to educate you in the fine art of true sexual completion. And when I am done with you, *cara,* you'll never again have to pretend to come—at least, not when you're with me."

"You're looking more ghastly by the minute, Caroline. Decidedly unwell, in fact. Are you feeling airsick? If so, I can have the steward bring you something to ease your discomfort."

The past had roared back to haunt her so vividly that it took a moment for Callie to resurface in the present, and realize the man observing her with mild concern now was the same man who'd humiliated her so thoroughly nine years before.

"No," she said, sipping her water to settle her queasy stomach. He, and not the jet, was the one making her feel ill. "I'm perfectly fine."

"And I'm hardly convinced! Did I perhaps strike a nerve? Nudge your conscience a little?"

How complacent he was, lounging carelessly on the settee next to her. How insufferably sure he wielded the upper hand.

"You reminded me how callous you are," she said. "I can't believe I'd forgotten."

"Callous?"

"That's right. Only a complete cad would hark back to one insignificant night buried in the past, when his brother and sister-in-law have been recently killed and left two children orphans."

"Hardly orphans, Caroline," he replied, not the least put out by her comment. "The children have grandparents and an uncle who care deeply about them."

"They have an aunt, too. And I care every bit as deeply about them as do you or your parents."

"Yes?" He stroked his jaw idly, and shot her a glance half-hidden beneath his thick, black eyelashes. "Unless I'm mistaken—and I seldom am, by the way—we've already had this discussion, not two days past. For reasons which defy explanation, you chose to be nothing more than an aunt-in-name-only to the twins, which makes your professed deep attachment to them rather difficult to swallow."

So here it comes, Callie thought. *At last we're getting down to the real heart of the matter.*

Somehow controlling her voice so as not to betray the apprehension rippling through her, she said, "I'd find that remark offensive, if it weren't so ludicrous. As it is, your arrogant assumption is nothing short of laughable. You have no idea what kind of connection I feel for those two children."

He shrugged, an elegant, carelessly dismissive gesture. "I repeat, it is hard to imagine you feel any connection at all, considering how little time you've spent with them."

"We lived half a world apart. Not exactly ideal for dropping by whenever the mood takes you."

He indicated the plush leather upholstery in the aircraft cabin, the fine crystal and china on the mahogany table, the monogrammed linen napkins. "Thanks to advances in aerospace engineering, not to mention comfort, the world grows smaller every day, Caroline."

"I lead a very busy life, and so did my sister."

"Indeed, yes." He nodded. "She traveled widely with my brother. He was heavily involved in the family automobile business, particularly as it pertained to our foreign dealerships."

"I know that. Vanessa and I kept in close touch, even if we didn't see each other often."

"Then you must also be aware that once Clemente and Gina started school, they weren't always free to accompany their parents. They stayed, instead, with their grandparents."

"And your point is?" Although she tossed the question at him nonchalantly enough, Callie sensed where the conversation was leading, and another ominous chill ran up her spine.

"That *my* mother and father have invested a great deal of time and effort in the well-being of their grandchildren." Leaning forward, he leveled a telling stare her way. "And that, in case you're wondering, is the *real* reason I chose to meet you in Paris. Because if you harbor any notion that you're going to disrupt the status quo, I intend to disabuse you of the idea before we touch down in Rome. I will not have my parents made any more upset than they already are."

Unfortunately that would probably be unavoidable, but Callie decided now was not a good time to tell him so. Instead, choosing her words carefully, she said, "I don't take pleasure in inflicting unnecessary pain on anyone, Paolo. It's not my style."

"My father will be particularly glad to hear it. My mother is suffering enough. He won't tolerate you, or anyone else, adding to her misery."

Ah, yes! The refined, reserved, decidedly suspicious Signor Salvatore Rainero thought all he had to do was snap his fingers and the rest of the world would gladly leap to accommodate his wishes.

Well, Ermanno hadn't, and nor was Callie about to do so. Not that she relished heaping more grief on the Raineros who were unquestionably suffering greatly, but they weren't the only ones with rights.

"Just so that we understand one another, Paolo, I won't be bullied, not by you *or* your father. I have just lost my only sister—"

"And I, a brother. That should not make us enemies."

"It seems not to make us friends, either, all your talk on the phone about my being family notwithstanding."

"There is family, and then there is family, Caroline. You would be making a mistake to interpret my words as being anything more than an attempt to offer you comfort and sympathy at a time when you need both. My loyalty, first, last and always, lies primarily with my blood relatives."

Goaded beyond caution, she shot back, "So does mine. Whether or not you like it, the twins are related as closely by blood to me as they are to you Raineros, and I promise you, I'm not about to take a back seat on your say-so. Far from it, Paolo. I intend to take a very active role in my niece's and nephew's future."

His jaw tightened ominously. Fixing her in a glance so lethal that she shivered, he said softly, "Then I was mistaken. We are indeed fated to be enemies—and you should be aware that I make a formidable foe, my dear. Ask anyone who's ever crossed me, and they'll tell you I take no prisoners."

CHAPTER THREE

IN CONTRAST to the bright day outside, the Rainero family crypt was dim, and terribly, terribly cold. The kind of cold that seeped into a person's bones. A dead cold. Even if the sun had been able to penetrate the thick stone of the outer walls, its heat would have been rendered ineffectual. Not even raging fire could touch the vault's smooth, thick marble floor and interior walls. They were impervious.

For Callie, this final part of the funeral proceedings was the most difficult to bear. The church in Rome had been filled with people, with human warmth and emotion. The swell of the organ, the scent of incense, the flowers, the ritual of prayer and hymns—they'd spoken of hope, of eternity. But here, on *Isola di Gemma,* with only the immediate family and a priest present, the finality of death hit home with a vengeance.

The small gathering of mourners formed a semicircle. Beside her, somber in a black suit and tie, Paolo stood with his head bent and his hands clasped at his waist.

Next to him, his mother wept silently, the tears running unchecked down her face. Her hands cupped the shoulders of the grandchildren in front of her, keeping them close, letting them know they were not alone.

Salvatore Rainero completed the group, his face unreadable, but Callie knew, if it had been left to him, she would not have been included in this final ceremony. Ever since her arrival at the Raineros's Rome apartment, he had remained civil, but distant.

Nor had he been the only one. The children had greeted her with faces shuttered with pain and eyes downcast.

"Hello," she'd murmured, her heart breaking for them. "Do you remember me?"

"You're our aunt from America," Gina replied politely, "and Mommy's sister."

"That's right. She brought you to visit me when you were three, and then again when you turned five." She knelt down and drew them into a hug, "Oh, my darlings, I'm so dreadfully sorry about what's happened. I never thought that the next time we were together…"

Her voice broke and she fought to hold back the tears. "You still have your nonna and nonno, and your Uncle Paolo, but I want you to know that you have me, too, and I love you very much."

They stood stiff as boards, tolerating her embrace because they were too well-mannered to push her away. But she felt their indifference anyway, and it hurt. It hurt badly.

In marked contrast, their grandmother had held out her arms and welcomed Callie with soft murmurs of sympathy. Lidia's kindness, when she had her own burden of grief to bear, had filled Callie with guilt.

Small wonder Paolo was so protective of his mother. She was a woman who gave first to others, and thought of herself last. That she would shortly face losing her grandchildren to a virtual stranger would be a devastating blow.

Not that Callie had any intention of denying either grandparent access to the twins, nor Paolo, either, come to that. Her reasons for claiming the children weren't based on malice or vengeance. They had to do with promises made over eight years before, when the children were newborn. But the

Raineros would soon discover what Callie had realized long ago: that even with the best intentions, maintaining close ties with someone who lived half a world away was difficult at best.

Of course, in her case, there'd been more to it than a matter of miles. At nineteen, the only way she'd been able to cope with her situation had been to put geographical distance between herself and her children.

When Vanessa and Ermanno had first suggested adopting the twins, it had seemed the best solution. Best for the children, at least, because what had Callie to offer them but a heart full of love and not much else?

Her sister and brother-in-law, on the other hand, could give them the kind of life every child deserved: a stable, comfortable home, the best education money could buy, and most important, *two* parents. Wasn't having both a mother *and* a father every child's birthright?

At fifteen weeks pregnant, and beside herself with worry and grief, Callie had thought so. But as time passed, she had grown increasingly less sure. They were *her* babies. She had conceived them and carried them in her womb almost to term.

With the sweat pouring down her face and no loving husband at her side to cheer her on, she gave birth to them. Heard their first tremulous cries. And when they were placed in her arms, they'd filled the huge empty hole in her heart left by the man who would never know he'd sired the two most beautiful, perfect children in the world.

Give them up? Not as long as she had breath in her body! But in the end, and even though it had nearly killed her, she'd made the sacrifice. For their sakes. Because they deserved better than what she could give them. Because she was only just nineteen and hadn't the wherewithal to support one child, let alone two. Because in allowing Vanessa and Ermanno to adopt them, they'd be with family and she'd know they'd always be cherished and loved. Because, because, because…

Who could have foreseen how tragedy would intervene and give her a second chance to take her rightful place in her children's lives? And it was her right, wasn't it? She *was* their birth mother.

Her gaze slid again to where they leaned against their grandmother, their little faces pinched with cold. Gina had cried herself to sleep last night and rebuffed Callie's attempts to comfort her. She'd wanted her nonna. Natural enough, Callie had reasoned, but that didn't soften the blow of rejection.

Clemente's sadness was more contained. He said little, but the loss showed in his eyes—a mute uncertainty where, two weeks before, there had surely been absolute faith in a parent's indestructibility. In his child's world, the elderly might sometimes die, but mothers and fathers never did.

A sudden sob welled up in Callie's throat. So much loss and sorrow for all of them, but especially the children. How could she justify tearing them away from everyone dear? How could she expect them to uproot themselves from the familiar, and settle in a foreign place, with a woman they barely knew?

And yet, how could she walk away from them again, when Vanessa had told her that, in their wills, she and Ermanno had named Callie the twins' sole guardian. Ignore her dead sister's wishes?

Promise me you'll take over, if something should happen to us. Lidia and Salvatore are past the age where they can keep up with two active children on a full-time basis, and Paolo is no more fit to be a father than he is to look after a puppy. But you, Callie, you're the perfect choice…the only choice…

Was she, after all? Had too many years gone by? Unsure of anything but a renewed sense of loss, Callie covered her mouth to suppress a sob.

A hand in the small of her back took her by surprise. "This is hard, I know, but lean on me, *cara,*" Paolo murmured, urging her close. "It will soon be over."

He was wrong. It would never be over. No matter how things were resolved, someone would end up being dreadfully hurt.

The jolt of compassion, of the urge to pull her into the shelter of his arms and protect her, shook Paolo to the core. He'd thought himself armed against her. Believed his alliance with his parents too invincible to be breached by the one person who could wreak utter havoc and heartbreak on his family.

After their confrontation en route from Paris to Rome, that Caroline was capable of just such action was a foregone conclusion. He'd seen the determination in the tilt of her chin, in the sparks shooting from her lovely blue eyes. Had heard the implicit threat behind her declared intent to play a very active role in the twins' future.

The insecure, anxious-to-please young maid-of-honor at his brother's wedding had turned into a steely-spined woman on a mission. That, since her arrival, she'd shown hints of a softer side, especially in her dealings with his mother and the twins, was something Paolo had done his best to ignore. She was, after all, intelligent enough not to alienate those she most needed as allies.

Yet all that notwithstanding, her smothered sob touched him profoundly. All at once, she was not a one-person army bent on war, but a sadly outnumbered creature badly in need of a defender. The quivering droop of her mouth, the sheen of unshed tears glimmering in her eyes, rendered her powerless.

She had walked alone, with her head held high, as the family made its way through the grounds to the crypt. But when the brief burial ceremony ended, he tucked her arm through the crook of his elbow and, disregarding the censure in his father's surprised glance, escorted her back to the villa.

"I remember the last time I was here," she said quietly, stopping on the limestone path to gaze at the sea, turning dark now as the sun sank lower. "I never dreamed that when I came back again, it would be to bury my sister."

He clasped her cold hand and squeezed it gently. "None of us did, Caroline."

A tear sparkled on her lashes, clung there a moment, then broke free to trickle down her cheek. "I miss her desperately. Even though we lived so far apart, she was always there when I needed her."

"I know. She loved you very much."

"Yes. Far more than you can begin to understand."

The rough edge of passion suddenly charging her grief, overlaid his sympathy with mistrust. In the last six years, as he'd gradually taken more control of the family business interests, he'd learned a lot about reading other people. His finely tuned instincts told him now that Caroline was hiding some sort of secret, one so onerous that even indirect reference to it left her eyes haunted with a sorrow that had to do with more than her sister's death.

Although he wished it could be otherwise, instinct also warned him to unearth that secret before she used it as ammunition in the custody battle he knew was in the offing. Anxious not to alert her suspicions, he said casually, "Before he takes the motor launch back to the mainland, Father Dominic will stay to commiserate with my parents, over a glass of wine. I can't speak for you, but I've had about all I can take of well-meant homilies on everlasting life. Right now, all I know is that I've lost a brother, and you're the only person who really understands what I'm going through. Will you take a walk through the gardens with me, before the sun goes down completely?"

"I'd rather be with the children."

He'd been afraid she'd say that, and had his reply all ready. "Jolanda will be supervising their early dinner. You'd be better off spending time with them later, before they go to bed."

"Who's Jolanda?"

"Our resident housekeeper. She and her husband live on the island and keep the villa prepared for whenever the family decides to visit. You don't need to worry, Caroline. She's known the children all their lives. They're very comfortable with her."

She shrugged, drawing his attention to how narrow and delicate her shoulders were beneath her black silk coat. "I suppose a little fresh air can't hurt. Anything's better than the scent of lilies. They used to be one of my favorite flowers, but all they are now is a reminder…."

"For me, too." He steered her along a side path that wound through the manicured grounds. "Ermanno never liked them, either."

"Were you and he very close?"

"Very, especially in the last few years. He was my mentor, my hero. If it hadn't been for him, I'd never have amounted to anything more than a rich man's idle son, with no ambition beyond catering to my self-indulgent lifestyle. I'd probably be dead myself, if it hadn't been for him."

He stopped, momentarily unable to continue as the absolute truth of his last statement hit home, and underlined yet again the extent of his personal loss. He could see the disgust on Ermanno's face, hear it in his voice, as clearly as if it were just yesterday that he'd taken Paolo by the scruff of the neck, shaken him like a dog with a rat, then flung him down in the dust.

You make me ashamed to admit you're my brother! You bring disgrace to the Rainero name, to everyone and everything you touch. What will it take for you to behave like a man, instead of a spoiled boy? How often will you break our mother's heart before she turns her face to the wall and gives up, because living with the fear of what you'll do next is more than she can bear? How many wrecked cars, and broken hearts, Paolo? How many fathers out for your blood, because of your treatment of their daughters? How many husbands seeking vengeance for their ruined marriages?

Well, this time the Rainero name and money won't get you off the hook. This time, you take your punishment, and it starts with facing our father. Did you know he had a heart attack when the police showed up at his door to tell him that you'd been arrested for brawling, and that he lies now in a hospital bed, with no guarantee that he'll survive? Do you even care?

For once, Paolo had had no glib answers. No pitiful excuses or shifting of blame. After a night in jail, with the dregs of Roman society keeping him company, he'd seen himself through Ermanno's eyes, and it had sickened him.

At his side, Caroline gave a start of surprise. "What do you mean, *you'd probably be dead yourself?*"

"I was not a model son," he said, soberly. "It took seeing my father clinging to life in a hospital bed, and knowing that I had put him there, for me to recognize the error of my ways."

"Now that you mention it, I remember Vanessa telling me he'd been ill. Some sort of cardiac problem, wasn't it?"

"Yes. Fortunately his willpower was stronger than his heart. He made an amazing recovery."

She made a face. "He's the type who would."

Too amused by her candor to take offense, he said, "You don't much like him, do you?"

"No," she said bluntly. "He never thought the Leightons were good enough to be associated with the Raineros."

"As he got to know your sister better, he changed his mind about that. He even went so far as to say she was like a daughter to him."

"I suppose he didn't have much choice *but* to accept her. At least she didn't put his life at risk, the way you say you did. Exactly how did you bring that about, by the way?"

"I publicly embarrassed him. He is a very proud man—too proud, some, including you, might say. But he was always a loving father, and it hurt him very deeply when I showed myself to be less than deserving of his affection, let alone his trust."

"You appear to get along well enough now. How did you redeem yourself?"

"I accepted responsibility for my actions. Instead of taking for granted the privileges that came of being the son of wealthy parents, I started earning them. I took my intended place in the family business."

"Sat behind a fancy desk in a fancy office, and dished out orders to underlings, you mean?" she said scornfully.

"No, Caroline. I started at the bottom, taking orders and learning from men often younger than myself, and worked my way into a position of authority only after I'd earned their respect. To coin a phrase often used in America, I smartened up."

"Better late than never, I suppose."

This time, he understood her tone, and the oddly closed expression on her face. "Yes," he said. "And that brings me to a subject we've both avoided mentioning, except briefly. I refer, of course, to the night of my brother's wedding."

She went to pull her arm free of his. "I really don't want to talk about that again."

Trapping her hand, he said, "I'm afraid we must. At the very least, allow me to apologize. I deeply regret having behaved the way I did. I'm afraid I treated you very unfairly that night."

"You did a lot more than that!" she cried heatedly, then clapped a hand to her mouth as if she'd accidentally bitten off the end of her tongue and was trying to stem the flow of blood.

Curious at her outburst, he said, "What do you mean, Caroline?"

"Never mind," she mumbled. "It doesn't matter."

"If it can cause you such distress all these years later, it certainly does." Tugging her to a stop, he turned her to face him. "What were my other sins?"

"Well, you're so proud of how smart you are, so figure it out for yourself, for heaven's sake!" All flushed and flustered, she glared at him. "It wasn't just that night, it was…it was the next day…and the next week."

Again, she seemed on the brink of some revelation which, at the last second, she thought better of. "But we were together just that one time, Caroline."

"Yes, and you couldn't have made it any clearer I'd better not expect a repeat performance!"

"Did you want one?" he asked, refusing to acknowledge the untoward stirring of desire such a prospect inspired.

"Absolutely not!" she said, vehemently. "But that was no reason for you to parade another woman under my nose."

"There were always other women in those days, *cara*."

"And you made it abundantly clear that I was just one of them."

"*Mea culpa!* My behavior was inexcusable." He cupped her chin, again forcing her to meet his gaze. "But without trying to shift blame, I feel justified in pointing out that you were not entirely without fault. You let me believe you were sexually experienced when, in fact, you were anything but."

"I'm surprised you even remember!"

"Such bitterness, so long after the fact, is out of all proportion to the incident," he said, regarding her thoughtfully. "What aren't you telling me, Caroline? What's been eating at you all this time, that you're still so full of anger toward me?"

She grew very still, and very pale. "Nothing. Seeing you again, here on this island, just brings everything back, that's all."

"What do you mean by 'everything'?"

"You…laughed at me. Made me feel inadequate…hopeless at sex."

"Then I should have been horse-whipped. You were a novice, yes, but you were enchanting, too. Ethereal in a gauzy confection of a gown that made you look like a princess."

And with skin as fine as purest silk…and flesh so firm and tight that a man would have had to be made of stone not to respond with blind, untempered passion…!

"Never mind trying to flatter me at this late date, Paolo," she said coolly. "I know I made a fool of myself."

A vicious streak of desire licked through his blood. "What if it isn't flattery? What if I'm finally admitting to a long-overdue truth? You're a beautiful woman, Caroline, and I don't believe for a minute that I'm the first man to tell you so."

She blushed and ran the tip of her tongue over her lower lip, drawing his eye to the delicious curve of her mouth, and leading him to wonder how many men had tasted it in the last nine years. She was more than beautiful; she was exquisite. Fine-boned, delicately featured…and seductively feminine, in a refined, understated way. How had he managed to dismiss all that, the first time around?

She held the collar of her coat close to her throat and shivered, although her color remained high. "I think I'd like to go inside now."

"Do I embarrass you by speaking so frankly?"

"No, but I'm surprised. We've been pretty much at odds ever since Paris. In fact, you've barely addressed a single word to me in the last four days, and now you're suddenly full of compliments. Forgive me if I find that rather suspicious."

"Perhaps," he said, "I'm having second thoughts about you. Perhaps I've misjudged you. Isn't that possible?"

"Possible." She tilted her shoulder in a tiny shrug. "But not probable."

"Then perhaps *you* misjudge me."

"Equally possible, I suppose."

"And just as improbable?"

"I'm willing to keep an open mind on the matter."

A curious lightness filled him, blurring the sharp edges of

his grief. Tucking her arm firmly in his again, he said, "Then I propose we call a truce, at least for now."

Thoughtfully she tipped her head to one side, a slight movement only, but it was enough to send her hair sliding over her shoulder in a fall of cool, blond silk. It took all his self-control not to catch it in his hand and let it spill between his fingers. "I guess it won't hurt to try."

He wasn't quite so sure. All at once, none of the truths to which he held fast seemed quite as absolute anymore.

"I have decided we shall remain here for another week," Salvatore announced, when the adults congregated in the day salon for coffee, after dinner. "This is a peaceful place, a place to start the healing."

"Another week?" Callie glanced from Lidia, to Paolo.

Neither seemed inclined to question the head of the household. *Typical,* she thought. *The master speaks, and the other two jump to obey his commands.* "I'd hoped to be back home by then."

Salvatore inspected her down the length of his aristocratic nose. "We have no wish to detain you, if you're in a hurry to leave us, Caroline."

"It's not that I'm in a hurry, Signor Rainero. You've been more than kind hosts and I'm grateful. However, I have obligations in San Francisco."

"And they are uppermost in your mind at this time, are they?"

How smoothly he managed to shift the context of her words and leave them cloaked in unflattering connotation! "Not at all," she said, meeting his gaze defiantly. "But I came here in a hurry and left others to take over my responsibilities at work. I hardly feel entitled to be absent any longer than is absolutely necessary."

"I understand." He waved his hand as if he were bestowing a benediction. "You are a career person. I confess I had forgotten. In my family, you see, the women are content to be wives and mothers. *That* is their career."

"What happens to those who don't want to marry or have children?"

"There is no such creature," he said, scandalized. "To have a husband and bear his children is an honor no self-respecting Italian woman would reject."

Callie couldn't let such an arrogant, outdated remark go unchallenged. "You're living in the dark ages, if you believe that!"

Paolo directed a look at his father and smiled. After a barely perceptible pause, Salvatore smiled, too, albeit thinly, and said, "I daresay I am a little out of touch. Tell me what it is you do, my dear, that you find so absorbing."

A little unnerved by his abrupt turnabout, she said, "I'm an architect."

"You must be very clever. What is your area of expertise?"

"I specialize in the restoration of Victorian houses."

"An admirable undertaking." Salvatore nodded approval. "We are not so different in our thinking, after all, in that we both recognize the importance of preserving the past. You must have spent years acquiring the knowledge to embark on such a career. Remind me again where you attended school."

"In the States," she replied evasively, suddenly uncomfortable at being the center of his probing attention. He could nod his handsome head and twinkle his dark eyes all he pleased, but he had a mind like a steel trap, and it was busily at work trying to put her off balance.

Nor was he the only one. Not about to let her get away with such a vague answer, Paolo said, "You're being much too modest, Caroline. As I recall, you won a scholarship to one of America's Ivy league universities. Smith, wasn't it?"

"Smith?" Salvatore sat up straighter. "Then it's small wonder you don't have time for marriage or children. It would be a pity to waste such a fine education. How long were you there?"

"I wasn't," she said, desperate to steer the conversation into safer channels. "And I didn't say—"

But Paolo cut her off. "You mean, you *didn't* go to Smith, after all? Why ever not?"

"What does it matter?" she shot back irritably. "The point I'm trying to make, if you'd do me the courtesy of letting me finish a sentence, is that I never said I didn't want children. In fact, I shortly hope to take on just such a responsibility, and very much look forward to doing so."

"You're getting married?"

"You're pregnant?"

Almost simultaneously, Salvatore and Paolo fired the questions at her.

"Neither," she said, aware that she'd painted herself into a corner. But there was no escaping it now, not unless she wanted to give the impression she didn't care what happened to her niece and nephew, and really, what was the point in delaying the inevitable?

Bracing herself, she said, as tactfully as she knew how, "I'm talking about Gina and Clemente. I know this probably comes as a shock to you, and please be assured I'm not trying to be deliberately hurtful, but I'm well able to provide a home for the twins in the States, and I'm wondering if their living with me might be good for them, at least for a while."

Lidia's coffee cup fell from nerveless fingers, and spread a dark stain over the sofa's pale silk upholstery. "Oh, Caroline, why would you say such a thing?" she wailed softly, her face crumpling. "Do you think we do not love them enough? That we will let them forget their mother?"

"No, Lidia," Callie said gently. "I know how dearly you love them. But I love them, too, and I believe I'm well-equipped to take their mother's place."

"The hell you are!" Salvatore roared, slamming his hand flat on the coffee table as Lidia buried her face in her hands. "You foolish woman, do you seriously think we will stand idly by and allow you to tear our grandchildren away from the only home they've ever known—and not only that, but to live with a woman who puts career before home and family?"

"Those are your conclusions, Signor Rainero, not mine. I wouldn't dream of relegating the children to second place. Just the opposite, in fact. I'd take an extended leave of absence from my work, and devote myself entirely to looking after them. As for tearing them away from you, that's utter nonsense and the furthest thing from my mind. I hope you'll visit them often. But I also believe a complete change of scene will benefit them at this time. I think learning something of their mother's country—learning its customs, seeing where she grew up, things like that—will help preserve her memory more indelibly for them."

"What you believe or think is of no consequence, young woman!" Salvatore informed her blackly.

"Father," Paolo intervened, shaking his head at his parent in what struck Callie as a distinctly cautionary manner, "be sensible and calm down before you have another heart attack. And you, Momma, dry your tears. Caroline is merely expressing an opinion to which she's obviously given careful thought, and frankly, what she's suggesting isn't entirely without merit. She *is* the closest substitute for Vanessa, after all, and could well fill her empty shoes better than you're willing to recognize."

But his father, purple with rage, was beyond sensible. "You're taking her side against us?" he bellowed. "Where's your sense of loyalty, man?"

"Exactly where it's always been, with you and the children. But they've suffered enough, without ending up being the pawns in an ugly tug-of-war, which is why I propose we direct our energies to finding a compromise that will satisfy everyone."

Lowering his voice, Salvatore said with such deadly emphasis that Callie's blood ran cold. "What need is there to talk of compromise when I know full well, as do you, that those children belong to us in a way that supercedes any claim this Johnny-come-lately aunt thinks she might have?"

"What if I can prove differently, Signor Rainero?" Callie said, goaded past all caution. "What if I plead my case before a family court judge, with evidence to support my claim?"

His smile resembled a death's head grimace. "Then prepare for a long and fruitless battle, my dear, because there is not a court in this country that will uphold a foreigner's right to interfere in the upbringing of children of Italian citizenship."

Sick with fear, she said, "Those children were born in the United States and are half American."

Cursing, Salvatore lunged up from the sofa, and strode to where she sat on the other side of the coffee table. "They have no ties to America," he thundered, looming over her threateningly. "They are Italian in every way that counts."

Paolo immediately intervened by pushing his father aside none too gently. "That'll do, *le mio padre!* You resolve nothing by browbeating our guest in such a fashion, and have said enough."

A timely reminder, Callie thought, realizing belatedly that she, too, had said more than enough. Salvatore wasn't the only one at fault. For all that she'd not intended it to be so, she'd allowed herself to be provoked into speaking rashly and inflicting pain, and for that she was sorry.

Paolo was right, she realized dazedly. There was no clear-cut solution to the situation in which she and the Raineros found themselves. They had to find a compromise, one which would not trample anyone's rights, least of all the twins'.

Her children's welfare had always dictated her choices. It

was why she'd made that promise to Vanessa in the first place. But she had neither the heart nor the stomach to enforce it for enforcement's sake. And nor, she acknowledged dazedly, would Vanessa expect her to do so.

Things had changed from what they'd been eight years ago, and so had the people—no, the *person,* Paolo, as closely involved as she herself. He was not the same man who'd loved and left her without a second thought. Perhaps, in view of that, what she'd perceived to be her inalienable rights weren't so inalienable, after all.

"Caroline?" Paolo approached her with outstretched hand. "I could use a little air, and so, I think, could you."

"Yes," she said, grateful for the suggestion.

A week ago, she'd been so sure she had all the answers. To find herself suddenly rethinking the whole issue of what was best for the children left her shaken and confused.

She needed to escape the tension in the room and clear her head. She needed to come to terms with her own abrupt change of heart and try to figure out exactly where that left her. And she could do neither pinned in Salvatore's inimical glare.

CHAPTER FOUR

"WHERE are we going?"

"Away from a confrontation grown too painful for all of us."

Callie's rational mind cautioned her not to trust every word that came out of Paolo's mouth, nor blindly follow where he led, just on his say-so. He might be a much more admirable man than he'd once been, but he was still a Rainero and, not five minutes ago, had admitted his first loyalty lay with his family. But the sure clasp of his fingers around hers warmed her soul; the compassion and, yes, the tenderness in his voice, soothed her battered spirit. In a house suddenly filled with such a wealth of enmity and mistrust, he was her only friend, because even Lidia must have lost sympathy for her now.

Taking her hand, Paolo led her out of a side entrance and along a path to a miniature two-story villa, some fifty feet removed from the main house, and hidden from it by a high hedge of flowering shrubs. Lights showed behind the draperies at the upper windows.

"Who lives here?"

"Jolanda and her husband."

"We're visiting them?"

"No. The night is mild. We'll take a drive around the island."

"I didn't know there were any roads here. I've only ever

seen the helicopter pad and the boat dock." Not that Callie in fact cared, one way or the other, but it was easier to focus on the insignificant than dwell on the scene they'd left behind: Lidia weeping and distraught, and Salvatore almost foaming at the mouth with rage and hatred.

"Hardly roads," Paolo said, sliding back a huge metal door on the main floor of the housekeeper's quarters, to reveal a late model Jeep parked inside a garage that also served as a handyman's workshop. "More like dirt tracks which can be accessed only by a four-wheel-drive vehicle like this, especially during the winter rains. Rather basic transportation, I'm afraid," he commented dryly, helping her climb into the passenger seat, "but it's the best I have to offer."

"Basic" was too kind a description. Once clear of the well-tended grounds of the villa, the Jeep bucked and jolted over the rocky terrain, sometimes veering frighteningly close to the edge of the cliff. Yet rather than fearing for her life, Callie felt safer and more comfortable than she had, back in the luxury of the villa. At twenty-four, Paolo had driven his low-slung luxury sports car like a maniac bent on self-destruction, but he handled the Jeep with masterful skill, and her pulse, which had raced erratically during the showdown with Salvatore, gradually settled back to normal.

"Thanks for rescuing me from your father's wrath," she ventured, the knots in her neck and shoulders lessening. "For a moment there, I thought he was actually going to hit me."

"My father would never strike a woman, Caroline."

"You could have fooled me. He was out of control."

Paolo debated her statement for a moment, then conceded grudgingly, "Sadly, I must agree with you. He hasn't been himself since we learned of the accident. But even if he'd so far forgotten himself that he'd attempted to touch you, I would have prevented it, even if it meant physically restraining him."

At that, a comforting warmth stole through Callie. Paolo

was a big, strong man, but so was Salvatore. Restraining him would not have been easy. "You'd have fought your father? For me?"

"I would fight any man threatening a woman," Paolo replied flatly. "But if you're asking me if I would embark on such a course lightly with my father, be assured I'd do so only as a last resort. A better solution by far was to defuse the situation by removing you."

"Why? Because I dared to tell him things he didn't want to hear?"

"Because it's not good for him to become so disturbed. His heart cannot take such stress. But seeing my mother hurt and suffering is never easy for him."

"I'm truly sorry I upset her. She's a remarkable, lovely woman, and it hurts me to know that I hurt her. But don't ask me to feel sorry for your father, Paolo. He's nothing but a bully when someone dares voice an opinion that doesn't coincide with his, especially if that someone happens to be a woman—and a Leighton, to boot."

"And again, I apologize for his behavior. He should not have treated you as he did."

"I don't want your apology, nor his, either," she said wearily. "All I ask is to be recognized as having the right to some say in the future of my niece and nephew."

"I give you my word that no one will deny you that right. One way or another, I'll find a way to keep everybody happy."

Before she could ask him how he expected to achieve the impossible, he turned off the main track and steered the Jeep down a narrow, less traveled path which ended on a small promontory overlooking the Adriatic.

"This last week has taken a toll on all of us," he said, bringing the vehicle to a stop on the lip of the cliff. "We're each dealing with grief in our own way, and liable to speak hasty words we immediately regret. My father's certainly guilty of that."

Shame-faced, she stared at her hands, clutched tightly in her lap. "No more than I am. I spoke out of turn. I should never have phrased my concerns in such a way that they came out as a threat."

"You mean, you aren't serious in wanting to take the children back to America with you?"

The moment of truth came out of the blue and left her gulping back a sob. "Oh, Paolo, I'd be lying if I said it's not what I've hoped for. But the more I see of them, the more I realize it's not about what I want. It's about what's best for them. And I'm no longer sure I have the answer to that."

"Perhaps none of us has," he said quietly, "which is why I brought you here. Sometimes, focusing on something else, even if it's only for a short time, helps restore our perspective and lead us to solutions we might never otherwise have considered."

"I wish I shared your optimism."

"There's no reason you can't, if you put your mind to it. Please, *cara,* try for a little while to forget about what the future holds, and simply enjoy this moment." He stabbed a finger at the Jeep's windshield. "Look out there, and tell me, did you ever see such a night?"

In truth, it was spectacular. Although the grounds of the villa were lushly planted with all kinds of tropical trees and flowers, there was little vegetation native to the island. By the light of the moon, hanging full and round and yellow just above the horizon, the bare landscape assumed an austere beauty that was almost ghostly.

Paolo leaned both arms on the steering wheel and gazed across the moon-dappled water. "Tell me about your life over the last nine years, Caroline. My mother has mentioned how very excited you were about attending Smith College, and that you spoke of it often, when you were here for the wedding. What made you decide against it?"

You did, she could have told him. *Because of you, all my dreams turned into nightmares….*

"You might as well take it off," he'd said, lifting one corner of her mangled maid-of-honor gown. "It's past saving."

An unforgiving sliver of moonlight confirmed his assessment. The full, filmy skirt sagging disastrously where it had torn away from the bodice, and the smear of blood near the hem, indicated she'd done a lot more than take an innocent stroll in the garden.

"And wear what?" she cried, appalled at the thought of having to account for how she'd managed to ruin a dress that had cost a small fortune, never mind everything else she'd done.

"Nothing, of course. We're going swimming."

"In the nude?" More rattled by the minute, she stared at him. "Someone might see us!"

"I doubt that will happen, but what if it did?" he returned carelessly. "I wouldn't be embarrassed."

No, he wouldn't. The way he peeled off the rest of his clothes until he stood before her as naked as the day he was born, was proof enough of that. And the way she stared, as if she couldn't get her fill of him, was nothing short of shameful.

"Well? Are you coming with me?" he said, standing straight and tall as a Roman god. "Or would you prefer to go back to the reception, looking like something washed up on the beach by the tide?"

Heaven help her, but at the sight of him, so beautifully male, so gloriously virile, that same prickling, giddy excitement swept over her afresh, and all she wanted was to go with him again down the illicit path of sexual discovery. Tomorrow was soon enough to worry about looking her mother in the eye, about offering explanations for behavior that was inexcusable. Tonight was made for first love.

Her white kid shoes, satin panties and fine lace stockings

already lay heaped on the cabana floor. Before she lost her nerve, she took off everything else and, worshiping him with her eyes, murmured breathlessly, "Of course I'm coming with you."

Watching her strip had aroused him. Touching himself, he fastened his gaze on her small, high breasts, then let it dip to the shadow at the juncture of her thighs. And again, that wicked rush of heat left her damp and molten, and aching for something just beyond her frame of experience.

He stepped close enough for his penis to nudge gently against her. "That's more like it," he murmured huskily, rolling her nipple gently between his forefinger and thumb.

A quiver puckered her flesh and brought it to a vibrant, electric life that left her entire body yearning ever more desperately for that elusive "something." She would have collapsed on the wooden floor and dragged him down on top of her, if he'd let her. But he backed away, teasing her with a smile, and catching her hand in his, ran with her across the sand to the water.

Once there, he dragged her, laughing, into the waves until they swirled around his chest. Only then did he pull her close and kiss her, tangling his fingers in her hair and driving his tongue deep into her mouth. Exhilarated, she returned his advances. His teeth were smooth, his lips warm, his tongue bold and hard, just like his erection.

She wound her arms around his neck, let her legs float up to encircle his waist. He slid his hands beneath her bottom, and with one finger, found the tiny bud of flesh hidden between the plump folds at her center.

It sprang to life like a wild thing, urgent and hungry for a satisfaction only he knew how to provide. Another slick, quick stroke from his clever finger, a little pressure in just the right place, and a lightning bolt shot through her.

"Oh…!" she gasped, and buried her face against his neck.

"*Si, bella*...now it begins for you," he murmured, and touched her again, more insistently.

This time, a hidden coil sprang free in a backlash of sensation so wicked that she'd have leaped clear of the water had he not locked his arm around her so firmly. A helpless moan, borne deep within her, escaped her lips and hung in the still night.

"*E ancora,*" he urged, tormenting her a third time...a fourth...a fifth, until, at last, her body responded with the elemental might of a sleeping volcano awakened at last.

She tensed, clenched her eyes shut, and sucked in a drowning, desperate breath as a wave of tremors, each more powerful than the last, gave way to an onslaught of earth-shattering spasms. Then the world as she'd known it exploded on her soft, high scream.

"I didn't know!" she breathed, long minutes later. "I had no idea...!"

"You do now, Caroline," he said, droplets of water running over his shoulders, and the heat of passion in his voice. "So let us proceed to the next phase of your education."

There was no question of returning to the villa after that. They didn't even make it back to the cabana. Right there, under the stars, with the warm Adriatic curling around them, they came together in a wild tangling of limbs and lips; of hands and tongues and fractured breathing.

To have him fill her completely, and know that they were joined not just in body, but in mind and heart as well, was surely the next best thing to heaven. "Oh, Paolo!" she whispered when, panting and depleted, they staggered ashore together. "You're a wonderful teacher!"

"And you, an exemplary student."

She turned her head and looked back along the beach. The faint sound of music drifted on the air. Just beyond the limestone outcropping, a rocket shot into the sky and cascaded back to earth in a free-fall of brilliant stars.

Fireworks, she realized. The wedding celebrations continued unabated, not in the least diminished by the absence of the best man and maid-of-honor. "I don't want to go back there tonight," she told him.

"Nor shall you," he replied. "There are showers in the cabana, and a supply of towels. We will stay there until the villa is asleep, and return before it awakes at dawn."

They bathed together, a playful, happy experience, laced with the promise of greater intimacy to come. Later, when she lay on a bed of thick white towels, he parted her legs and put his mouth on her. Stroked her with his tongue. And after her initial shocked reaction, she reveled in the forbidden pleasure he gave, awash in wonder at the sensuality she'd never guessed was hers to enjoy.

If their first time together had been embarrassing, and the second amazing, the third offered an unequivocal taste of sheer paradise, such that, when he collapsed on top of her, spent, she couldn't help herself. "I love you, Paolo!" she gasped brokenly. They were the *only* words to describe the depth of emotion rolling over her.

For the longest time, he didn't reply. Seemed unable to look at her, even. When he finally spoke, it was to say with calculated indifference, "It grows late, *tesoro,* and you are tired. We should sleep for a few hours. Regain our strength for yet another pleasurable encounter."

When he awoke, though, just as the sun crept over the sea, Paolo was no more interested in making love to her than he was to remain cooped up on the island a second longer than he had to.

"We had fun, yes?" he said, climbing into his clothes. "But the wedding fever is over, and it's back to life as usual. For you, that means returning to America and your fine university."

"Don't you believe in marriage, Paolo?"

"For some people, perhaps."

His shrug spoke volumes. But she was a devil for punishment, and couldn't let go gracefully. "But not for you?"

"The world is full of beautiful women, Caroline," he said cheerfully. "How can I be expected to choose just one?"

"Do you even believe in love?"

"But of course! I love women—*all* women." He smiled his charming, devil-may-care smile. "I am Italian. I love *love!*"

She tried to smile back, and started to cry instead as all her hopes went up in smoke. "I thought I was special, but I'm just the latest in a long line of willing conquests, aren't I?"

"Don't do this, *cara,*" he said, rolling his magnificent brown eyes. "Don't spoil our glorious time together with tears and recriminations."

"I suppose I should be flattered you spared me one whole night. Silly me, to have thought it was the beginning of something lasting, something b...beautiful!"

"Ah, Caroline...!" Briefly he touched her face and let his fingers linger almost regretfully at her mouth, before stepping firmly away. "You see your world through rose-colored spectacles, *cara mia,* whereas I learned long ago that mine is painted in ugly shades of gray."

If she hadn't known then that she meant nothing to him, he drove the point home a few days later. On the Thursday before they were to fly back to the U.S., Callie and her mother stayed overnight in Rome, with the Raineros. The next morning, just as they stepped out to the street where a taxi waited to take them to the airport, Paolo drove up in a fire-red Ferrari.

He had a woman with him; a sultry, voluptuous, dark-haired beauty in a skimpy top and a thigh-high skirt, who sat so close beside him that she was practically in his lap. But when he went to kiss her, she laughed, pulled away and rolled her tongue provocatively over her full, red upper lip.

Suddenly Callie saw herself through his eyes—a pathetically naive girl with a bad case of puppy love. No wonder he hadn't wanted to continue their affair. He liked his women sophisticated, sure of themselves and elusive. The more difficult the chase, the better he liked it.

She was so far out of her league, it was laughable. Rather than being the object of his desire, she'd been an amusing bit player. Someone to laugh about with his male friends. A convenient and willing body to keep him entertained until a better prospect showed up.

If only it could have ended then, with her humiliation complete, her heart in pieces, but her future, at least, intact. But he was not to be so easily dismissed. A month later, she discovered she was pregnant, and all that bright and shining opportunity she'd thought was hers for the taking, lay in shambles.

There would be no Smith College, no graduation summa cum laude. She had let down all the people who believed in her: her mother, who'd been so proud of her scholastic achievements; the board of governors at her private school, who'd awarded her their highest scholarship prize; her headmistress, who'd written such a glowing letter of recommendation to the college on her behalf.

And Vanessa.

"You're *what?*" she exclaimed, after Callie confided in her sister. Their mother was away at the time, visiting a cousin in Florida, but Vanessa and Ermanno were in New York on the first leg of their year-long honeymoon-cum-business tour, and drove up to spend the weekend with Callie, who'd stayed home. "Good grief, Callie, I didn't know you were seeing somebody. Have you told Mom?"

"No. I found out just before she left for Florida. She'd have canceled the trip if she'd known."

Still reeling, Vanessa said, "I can't believe it! You always claimed you didn't have time for a steady boyfriend. When...*who?*"

It had taken all Callie's courage to mumble, "Your brother-in-law. The day you got married."

"Paolo?" Vanessa clapped a hand to her mouth, aghast. "My God, Ermanno will kill him!"

"Ermanno can't know. Don't tell him, please!" Callie begged.

But Vanessa stood firm. "I'm not keeping a secret like this from my husband. He has a right to know."

Outraged when he heard, Ermanno's first reaction was that he'd see to it Paolo did the honorable thing and married Callie.

She flatly refused to consider the idea. "I'm not compounding one grievous mistake with another. Marriage is out of the question, even if you could drag Paolo to the altar, which I highly doubt."

"I'm afraid you're right," Ermanno said, after a moment's reflection. "The last thing you need is a husband incapable of fidelity. We must find another solution, one which will keep this shameful secret from my father. It would destroy him, to learn that his favorite son has disgraced our family in such a way."

He spoke without rancor, and when Callie remarked on it, shrugged philosophically and said, "I accepted long ago that, in my father's eyes, Paolo is the golden boy who can do no wrong. I'm not saying my father doesn't love me, too, but my brother…it's different with him, and that's just the way it is."

"Your father sometimes doesn't use the sense he was born with," Vanessa declared, planting a loving kiss on her husband's cheek. "But I, thank goodness, do!" Then, turning to Callie, she said, "We'll figure out a way to help you, honey. I take it you've seen a doctor?"

"Yes. He pointed out my choices—abortion, adoption or keeping the baby."

"And?" Vanessa eyed her anxiously.

"I can't terminate the pregnancy. I couldn't live with myself, if I did."

Visibly relieved, her sister asked, "What about adoption?"

"Oh, Vanessa!" Callie's eyes overflowed again. "I don't think I could go through with that, either. Giving my baby away to strangers—" She stopped to mop her tears. "I'm so ashamed. How am I ever going to face Mom."

"Never mind the shame," Vanessa declared. "The point is, pregnancy isn't something you can keep secret for very long. Soon, everyone will know, including Mom."

"No! I could move away. Get a job. Save my money—"

"There is no need to worry about money," Ermanno said quietly. "That is one thing I *can* do something about."

"And you have to tell Mom, Callie. She'll be shocked, of course, but you know she'll stand by you. Maybe, with her help, you'll be able to keep the baby."

"I don't think I can stand to see the disappointment in her eyes," Callie said miserably.

As it turned out, she didn't have to. Tragically, on the drive home from Florida, their mother was killed in a head-on collision in North Carolina. She never knew she was about to become a grandmother.

The hot splash of tears on her face drew Callie back to the present—that, and Paolo's voice, low and concerned, observing, "What did I say to make you cry, Caroline?"

"You asked me why I didn't go to Smith," she said, swiping her fingers over her cheeks. "If you must know, it was because of my mother's death."

How plausibly the lie rolled off her tongue! Accepting it without hesitation, he said, "Ah, yes! I remember now that she died not long after Ermanno married Vanessa."

"That same summer. My father left us when I was six and Vanessa eleven, so for most of my life it had been just my mother, my sister and I. Then, in the space of two months, I was alone."

Except for your babies, of course!

That had been the next shock to hit her.

"Definitely twins," the obstetrician to whom her doctor referred her had declared confidently. "Two for the price of one, young lady. You're going to have to take very good care of yourself for the next five months. We don't want a premature delivery."

Oh, the blistering shame, to be the youngest daughter of the late, respected Audrey Leighton, president of the Junior League, pillar of society. To be pregnant and unmarried—with twins. Oh, God! Oh, God!

"You weren't really alone. You still had your sister, and Ermanno, too."

Oh, yes. More than you can begin to know! "I seldom saw them. They were traveling all over the world for the better part of a year."

"So they were—until Vanessa was put on bed rest because of her pregnancy. They stayed in California then, until after the twins were born, didn't they?"

"Yes," she said, with guilelessly misleading honesty.

"And you were there for the birth?"

Callie stared fixedly at the moonlit sea, hating that she had to mouth another lie, albeit by omission. "Yes."

"My mother planned to be there, also, but the babies came almost a month earlier than expected."

"Mmm-hmm." Actually only ten days early, thanks to the excellent care Callie had received. But Vanessa and Ermanno had planned their story carefully, to avoid just such a situation as Paolo described.

He shifted in his seat and then, shockingly, stroked the back of his hand down her cheek. "Ah, Caroline," he said softly. "I see how it hurts you, that you were there to welcome the children into the world, and yet could not be here, to see them grow up."

"You don't know the half of it," she cried, scrunching her

eyes shut against the painful images forcing their way to the forefront of her mind.

To give birth, to hold her babies close to her heart and smell their sweet, newborn smell—and then, ten days later, to let them go? There were no words to describe the emptiness, the agony.

Even after all this time, the picture remained as painfully sharp as if it had happened just yesterday: Vanessa, wearing a yellow dress and matching jacket, Ermanno in a pale gray suit, and each of them holding a tiny bundle wrapped in a soft white blanket.

You know we couldn't love them more, if they were our very own, Callie.

Never fear that they will want for anything, Caroline. They will have the best that money can buy.

Before stepping into the waiting limousine, Vanessa turned one last time to Callie. *We'll give them brothers and sisters. They'll be part of a big, loving family—and so will you, Callie. You'll be their darling aunt.*

But the other children never materialized. Vanessa had been unable to conceive. *Oh, Callie!* she had wept. *If it weren't for you, I'd never have known the joy of being a mother. Thank you so much, darling, for the gift you gave us.*

"Then tell me all of it," Paolo urged. "Tell me what it is that haunts you with such sorrow."

"My sister died last week," she said, choking back a sob. "Isn't that enough?"

Sliding his arm around her shoulder, he pulled her close and cupped her chin, forcing her to look at him. "There's more," he insisted. "I hear it in your voice. I see it in your eyes. What is it you're holding back? Please, Caroline, let me help you."

"You?" Her laugh verged on the hysterical. "I hardly think so!"

"Why? Because, the first time I held you in my arms, I was

too foolish to realize your true worth?" He expelled a huge sigh of frustration. "That was a long time ago, *cara.* Trust me when I tell you, I've changed for the better since then."

Temptation nibbled at the edges of her resolve. Quickly, before it gained too powerful a hold, she replied, "Easy for you to say, Paolo, but where's the proof?"

"Here." He tapped a fist to his chest. "I admit that when I met you in Paris, I viewed you as a threat to my family, and was prepared to squash you flat at the first hint of sabotage. But I've watched you, this last week. I've seen your kindness to my mother, the way you sit with her and try to comfort her when your own heart is also breaking. I've seen how patient you are with the children, how loving, even though, more often than not, they rebuff your overtures."

His hand strayed down her throat, stole around her neck. "If it were within your power to do so, I believe you would change places with Vanessa, just to give them back their mother. Yet something more than that is eating you alive. I *know* it, and it worries me, even as my heart tells me you're incapable of sinister motives."

"*My* heart hears your words and wants to believe them," she countered tremulously, "but my head tells me actions are what count."

"Then let your head be the best judge of this," he said, and before she could guess his intent, let alone utter a protest, his mouth came down on hers and fastened there in a burst of heat that set her blood on fire.

CHAPTER FIVE

SHE'D felt faint stirrings of desire with other men since he'd initiated her into the art of love, nine years before. Kinder, less dangerous men. More sympathetic and deserving men. But always, Callie had withheld herself, even if her current love interest hadn't known it. When it came right down to that moment of ultimate surrender, she hadn't been able to let go. Not once, since the night she'd conceived Paolo's children, had she permitted herself the freedom to respond without reservation or inhibition.

But if she'd spent the intervening years suppressing her sexual urges, Paolo had clearly spent the same amount of time fine-tuning his. The once-reckless womanizer had matured into a virtuoso seducer whose finesse laid instant waste to her resistance.

The very second his mouth touched hers, all thought of self-preservation fled her mind. With just a kiss, he turned her world on its ear, and nothing mattered but to prolong the pleasure of being in his arms again; of awakening after a long and arid sleep, and *feeling,* with every cell in her body, every beat of her heart, the sweet, sharp trickle of desire permeating her blood. Without a moment's pause, she was ready to sell her soul all over again, if that's what it took to satisfy the raging hunger he inspired.

Her lips softened, parted. How else could she drink in the essence of him? When his tongue trespassed beyond the bounds of friendship and entered the forbidden territory of lovers, she held it prisoner, drawing it ever deeper into her mouth.

She cradled his cheek. Let her fingers steal up to knot fiercely in his thick, black hair. She swayed against him, arousing both him and herself by brushing her nipples lightly against his chest.

His hand skated from her throat to her ribs, and settled urgently, possessively, at her hip. For the first time in what seemed like eternity, she again experienced that scalding rush of heat between her legs. Sensed the distant tremors gathering strength within her, forerunners of a starving passion that would be satisfied with nothing less than complete fulfillment.

How disastrously it all might have ended, had he not exercised some restraint, was anybody's guess. But again, with a discipline his younger self had never shown, he pulled them both back from the brink. "Forgive me, Caroline," he said hoarsely, shoving her almost roughly into the far corner of the passenger seat. "I should not have done that."

Dazed, disappointed, she swiped her hand across her mouth and injected a hard-won note of outrage into her reply. "Why did you then?"

"I couldn't help myself." He hesitated, and if she hadn't known him to be the most confident man she'd ever met, she'd have thought him unsure he should utter his next words.

At length, though, he went on, "I find myself drawn to you. You touch me—against my will, I might add—with your self-contained grief. I see the way you swallow when the pain almost gets the better of you, and I wish I could comfort you. But I forfeited that right a long time ago, and of the many things I regret having done, it's that I've given you no reason to trust me now."

Another silence, this one full of brooding frustration, before he burst out savagely, "*Dio,* if it were within my power, I would have us meeting here for the first time, with no painful history to sour your view of me!"

"We were both young and foolish, Paolo," she said, an unsettling stab of guilt attacking without warning. She was the injured party, the one who'd given up everything—or so she'd told herself these many long years. Yet in line with other recent self-insights, as she watched him, listened to him, she suddenly wasn't quite so sure.

"But I was the greater transgressor." Fleetingly his hand ghosted over her hair and down her face. "You were little more than a child, Caroline, and so anxious to please that it disgusts me to remember how I took advantage of you. If I had a daughter, I would kill the man who dared to treat her, as I treated you."

Tell him! Say the words: You do have a daughter, Paolo, and a son, as well! Then let the chips fall where they may. Dare to believe that the truth can indeed set a person free.

The urge to confess rose, as strong and surprising as her earlier guilt. She had to bite her tongue not to give in to what was surely the ultimate folly. A moment's lapse in judgment could cost her everything because, no matter what he might say now, his repentance would surely turn to outrage when he learned the secret she'd kept from him all this time.

"You do not answer me," he said, a world of weary regret in his voice.

"What do you want me to say? That I forgive you?"

"No. That's asking for far more than I deserve."

His candor was killing her! Too ashamed of her hypocrisy to look him in the eye, she stared again at the swath of moonlit sea. "No, it's not. In the last week, we've both learned that life's too short to waste it bearing grudges. So let's forgive each other, Paolo, for the mistakes we've *both* made."

"What are yours?" he asked, with just a trace of humor in

his tone. "That you were too beautiful for your own good? Too sweetly appealing for mine?"

Humbled yet again by his self-derision, she said, "I chose to be a stranger to my own flesh and blood, just as you accused me of doing. I stayed away from my niece and nephew, when I should have made an effort to grow closer to them."

"You're here for them now, *cara.*"

Yes, but deep in her heart, she was terribly afraid she'd left it too late. Her children didn't want to know her.

They turned to Lidia to dry their tears and sing them to sleep. They ran to Paolo when it hit them that Ermanno could no longer be there for them. Even Salvatore occupied a special place in their hearts, regardless of Callie's belief that he was far removed from the typically warm, loving Italian patriarch they deserved. When all was said and done, the Raineros were her children's true family, and she had only herself to blame for that.

Blinking away the persistent threat of tears, she said, "I mean nothing to them. You said so, yourself."

"They are afraid to love you."

Another wave of pain engulfed her. "*Afraid?* Why?"

"Because they have learned too early what it is to have the very foundation of their lives knocked out from under them. As they see it, their parents have abandoned them, and so might you. You are kind and tender with them, everything a loving aunt should be. But they are not, I fear, willing to risk another loss, so soon after the first."

"So how do I rectify that?"

"By not turning their world upside-down with impossible demands. Do not ask them to open their hearts to you, just because you happen to be their mother's sister. Don't be in too big a hurry to rush back to America. Rather, stay here in Italy long enough to earn their trust. Do that, and their affection will follow."

"That could take months."

He shrugged. "So? You already said you're prepared to take a leave of absence from your work. Have you had second thoughts, and decided Gina and Clemente aren't worth such a sacrifice?"

"Of course not! But—"

"But you have your own life, one you share perhaps with a lover?"

"No."

"Then what's so important about your schedule that everything has to conform to it, regardless of how it might affect other people's?"

Seeing herself through his eyes, she cried passionately, "You don't understand!"

"Then make me," he said. "You say you want what's best for our niece and nephew—"

"I do! I want to give them the kind of security that comes from knowing that they are deeply and irrevocably loved, even though their parents have died."

"Which is exactly what I also want for them. So why, if we're in agreement, are we fighting each other?"

"I don't know!" she cried, frustration spilling over. He knocked all the starch out of her convictions with his powerful line of reasoning. "I can't think straight when you badger me like this!"

"Is that what I'm doing, Caroline? Badgering you?"

No, you're reinforcing a whole host of self-doubts about what I thought were entrenched beliefs in my rights, and I can't deal with that, especially not with you sitting so close beside me that I forget to be prudent.

"Am I?" he said again, running his knuckles along her jaw in a caress so tender that it undid her.

Her vision blurred. "No," she said, blinking furiously. "I'm feeling overwhelmed, that's all."

"Understandable." Another pause followed, this one humming with a different kind of energy, before he said thoughtfully, "Given our common goal, can we not find a way to work together, instead of in opposition?"

Tamping down an improbable surge of hope, she said warily, "Exactly what is it you're proposing, Paolo?"

"That you give me one year. Put your career on hold and take that leave of absence and live here. With me."

"With *you?* You mean, in your house?"

"Exactly. At present, I own an apartment, but for the children's sake, I would buy a villa on the outskirts of Rome. A place with a garden where they could play—one close to where they lived with their parents, so that they could attend the same school, and keep the same friends. In other words, I would make a home for them—and you."

"You can't possibly be suggesting that the four of us would all live under the same roof?"

"Why not?"

"Because your father wouldn't allow it, for a start!"

"My father does not dictate my choices, Caroline. I am my own man."

She didn't doubt that for a moment. "Perhaps. But he'd never accept my place at your side."

"He'd have no choice *but* to accept you, if you were my wife."

"You're suggesting we get *married?*" This time, there was no controlling her spiking blood pressure.

"Yes," he said calmly, as if proposing marriage out of the blue was as common an everyday occurrence as brushing his teeth.

"But you don't love me!"

"Nor do you love me. But we both love the children, do we not?"

"Well…yes."

"Then is it not worth trying to give back to them a little of what they've lost—a home, two people who love them, a semblance of normality?"

To be his wife, to share a home with him and their children…had this not been the stuff her dreams were made of, for longer than she cared to admit? And yet, to grasp them now, on the strength of a whim, an impulse, was surely courting heartbreak all over again.

Quickly, before her foolish heart led her astray a second time where he was concerned, she said, "With a marriage in name only? I don't think so, Paolo!"

"Nor do I. Such marriages stand no chance of succeeding."

By then too confused to be delicate, she said bluntly, "Are you suggesting we sleep together?"

With enviable aplomb, he replied, "Why not? I admit, intimacy coupled with love makes for the *best* bedfellows, but between compatible, consenting adults, intimacy alone can nurture a closeness they might otherwise never know."

"What if it doesn't?"

"Then they part as friends and go their separate ways, which is why I ask you to give me a year. If, at the end of it, we agree we cannot make the marriage work, we will end it."

"And exactly how does that help the children?"

"It gives them a breathing space, a time to heal, among people who care about them enough to put their personal ambitions aside. At the same time, it allows them the chance to get to know you, which cannot be a bad thing if, as you say, you want what is best for them—because you surely must agree, no child can have too large a loving family."

"I do agree. It's this other thing you're suggesting…this business of…of sex…."

"I've taken you by surprise, I know, Caroline, and I don't expect an answer from you tonight. All I ask is that you consider my proposal."

Consider it? Good grief, it was all she could do not to grab hold of it with both hands before he changed his mind! But his businesslike approach cooled her enthusiasm. He was proposing a marriage of convenience, even if it did include bedroom privileges, and she'd be a fool to forget that. The odds that they could make a success of such an arrangement were dim at best.

So, matching his detachment, she said, "I suppose that can't hurt."

"My father wants us to stay here another week, but I suggest we make it two. That should give you enough time to reach a decision, shouldn't it?"

"I can't imagine it'll take me that long."

"But if you say yes, as I'm hoping you will, the extra time will give the children the chance to get used to the idea of us being a family, before too many changes take place. Then, once they've accepted the idea, we can return to Rome, and concentrate on finding a place to live."

"That makes sense, I suppose," she said, and wondered how he managed to make what was surely a rash, improbable idea seem so utterly sane and workable.

"You were gone a long time, Paolo," his mother said, coming out to where he leaned against the terrace balustrade, nursing a snifter of brandy. "Your father is in bed already."

"And why aren't you, Momma?" he asked fondly, noting the long silky robe she wore over her nightgown, and the embroidered satin slippers on her feet. "Aren't I bit past the age where you have to wait up, to make sure I get home safely?"

"I'm too worried and sad to sleep. First, Caroline told us she'd like to take the children back to America with her—"

"We've known all along that was a possibility. It shouldn't have come as too much of a surprise."

"No, but it still came as a shock to hear it put into words

so plainly. Then, after the pair of you left the house, I found the twins huddled at the top of the stairs, with their arms around each other. They were very upset and confused. I'm afraid, with their grandfather's shouting, they heard more than was good for them."

"My father was out of control. People on the mainland probably heard him. Were you able to reassure them?"

"I tried, but they heard Caroline, too. Their English is too good, Paolo. They understood every word that was spoken, and they're frightened. Everything they've always been able to count on is crumbling around them."

A sigh shook her slight frame, and Paolo realized that Ermanno's death had taken an even greater toll on her reserves than had first been apparent. The silver in her hair grew more noticeable every day. The spring had gone from her step, and she'd lost a shocking amount of weight.

Nor was grief the only culprit. She was exhausted. Even with Jolanda's help here on the island, and with the nanny, Tullia, standing by in Rome, caring for the twins exacted too heavy a toll on a woman of their grandmother's years.

"My heart bleeds for Caroline," she continued sadly. "She's in an impossible position, even if she doesn't yet realize it. She loves those children, and there's no question but that their lives would be enriched by having her be a part of them. But even if she could force the issue by taking them to live with her in America, what good would it do, if they ended up hating her for it?"

"No good at all. Technically they *are* half-American, as Caroline says, but in their hearts and outlook, they are as Italian as I am. Their true home is here, and always will be, regardless of who wins this battle of guardianship. Not only that, they're no longer babies. We speak of rights as if they're exclusive to adults only, but the children have their rights, too, and they deserve to be heard."

Another deep sigh escaped his mother. "Oh, Paolo! How are we ever going to resolve the difficulties facing us?"

"We'll find a way, Momma. In fact, I might already have come up with a solution that will make everyone happy."

His mother stepped closer, her face illuminated with sudden hope. "What kind of solution? Oh, tell me, please! I crave hearing some good news, for a change."

"No," he said. "You'll have to be patient a little longer. It is too soon."

Too soon for Caroline, and in all truth, too soon for him. The idea of marriage had struck him out of the blue, and before he'd had time to consider the wisdom of it, he'd proposed. And why? Because of a kiss that had been equally unplanned, yet one which had awoken in him a hunger not easily assuaged in the usual way. Rather, he'd been reminded of that long-ago night when he'd taken an innocent virgin and almost lost his heart in the process.

The depth of his feelings had terrified him then, and it terrified him now. At eighteen, she'd been a girl on the brink of life; one who deserved better than a man unprepared to accept responsibility for anything but his own pleasure and pursuits, and so he'd turned away from her.

Now, she was a woman and, in the space of a few days, she'd shown his life for what it really was: empty and superficial. Granted, at a professional level, he took pride in his accomplishments, and had believed that to be satisfaction enough. But because of her, he'd suddenly glimpsed the fulfillment of a deep-seated personal need that he hadn't known existed. Plainly put, she exemplified all the things he'd once thought he'd never want.

Children, marriage, a place to call home—they'd taken on different meaning, this last week, yet with one kiss, she'd made them appear not merely appropriate at such a grief-ravaged time, but eminently desirable, too.

He was not the twins' father, nor was Caroline their mother, but given the will to make it happen, together they could fill the void left by the tragic absence of parents, far better than either could hope to achieve alone. Like her, though, he needed time to adjust to the idea; to swing his mind set around from that of unattached bachelor, to family man. And he needed peace and quiet and solitude to do so.

"You should try to get some sleep, Momma," he said, urging her inside the villa. "You're worn-out."

"Sleep?" She passed her hand over her face in a gesture of utter despair. "How can I sleep, with so much gone wrong in my family?"

"By allowing someone else to carry the load, for a change." Taking her arm, he walked her to the foot of the staircase. "Put your worries aside, go to bed, and leave everything to me."

He watched as she took the stairs one at a time. Seeing how slowly she moved, how she clutched the bannister and paused occasionally to catch her breath, reinforced his determination. He would not wait until he buried his mother as well, before he took the necessary steps to bring closure to his family's distress.

When she at last reached her bedroom and closed the door, he returned to the terrace to finish his brandy, and pick up where he'd left off with his earlier musings. He'd always believed a man was responsible for directing his own destiny, but that he'd stumbled across such an ideal solution of how best to fill the hole left by Ermanno's and Vanessa's deaths, struck him as nothing less than serendipity.

Admittedly he entertained some reservations about his proposal. Try though he might, he couldn't quite shake the feeling that Caroline harbored a secret of such momentous proportions that it might one day hurt his family. But that merely made marrying her that much more urgent. As her husband, he'd be in a position to effect some damage control.

There were other advantages, too. Whatever faults she

might have, one thing remained unalterably clear: she was devoted to the twins, and ideally suited to share the responsibility of looking after them.

Furthermore, she was unattached, as was he. Even if he'd been seriously involved with another woman, he'd heard enough horror stories to make him reluctant to ask a stranger to step in as surrogate mother to his brother's children. But Caroline was family. Her blood ran in the twins' veins, just as thickly as his. Whatever their differences, in this one matter they were united.

If she was secure enough in the marriage, if he could make it so good between the two of them that she'd want to stay when the year was up, wouldn't that be enough to neutralize whatever threat he feared she posed for his family? Wouldn't it, in fact, be the best possible outcome for *everybody,* including the children?

Last, of course, there was the kiss—another unforeseen event which had affected him deeply. In that kiss, he'd tasted something of the ingenue he'd so carelessly cast aside nine years ago, and in his world, that kind of innocence was a rare commodity.

He hadn't asked her if there'd been other lovers since him, because he hadn't needed to. It had been there for him to see in her dazed surprise; in the nervous fluttering of her pulse, and her startled, uncertain gaze. A woman of experience did not respond so skittishly to a kiss, or to the suggestion of married intimacy.

And yes, there was that, too. Sharing a bed. Seeing her naked in the tub. Touching her in the privacy of their room, with lamplight casting golden shadows over her cool, smooth skin. Losing himself in her soft, warm folds, under cover of night.

The mere thought was enough to leave him hard and aching.

A sound penetrated the night; a thin, pitiful wail drifting

down from one of the bedrooms behind him. Leaving his glass on the stone balustrade, he raced inside to investigate.

He was halfway up the stairs when he heard it again, coming from Gina's room, at the end of the upper hall. The door to his parents' suite remained closed, a sign that his mother had managed to fall asleep, after all, but Caroline's stood ajar. Following the thread of light spilling over the floor from the room next to hers, he found her bent over Gina's bed, attempting to gather the child into her arms and soothe her.

"Hush, darling," he heard her murmur. "It was a bad dream, that's all. You're safe now."

But Gina was inconsolable. "I want my mommy," she sobbed.

"Mommy's gone to heaven, but you have me, precious," Caroline crooned. "You'll always have me. I'll never leave you, I promise."

For a moment, he thought Gina was going to accept her. Just briefly, she rested her tearstained face against her aunt's shoulder. Then she saw him standing on the threshold, and she pulled away, stretching out her arms to him, instead.

"Go away!" she cried to Caroline. "I don't want you, I want my Zio Paolo."

Caroline recoiled as if she'd been stabbed in the heart. Without a word, she rose from the edge of the bed to make room for him, and started toward the door.

"Don't leave, Caroline," he begged, catching her by the arm as she passed. "Let's do this together."

But, "You heard her," she said. "She wants you, not me."

"She wants her mother, *cara mia,* and her father, too. I'm her third choice only."

"And I'm nothing," she muttered brokenly, tearing free from his hold, and ran blindly from the room.

He let her go because there was misery enough in the

atmosphere at that moment, and Gina needed comfort. But once the child had settled down again, he stopped outside Caroline's room and knocked.

She didn't answer, but she'd left it too late to pretend she was asleep. He'd already noticed the seam of light showing under her door, and heard her crying softly.

"You might as well answer, Caroline, because I'm coming in, anyway," he said.

After a second of heavy silence punctuated only by an occasional sniffle, she spoke, her voice still muffled with tears. "What for? To rub my nose in the fact that my niece would rather deal with the devil himself, than with me?"

"Let me in, and we'll talk about that," he replied, not about to engage in any sort of discussion with a closed door between them.

She cracked it open an inch. "What's the matter?" she inquired bitterly as, taking advantage of the moment, he lost no time stepping quickly into the room and closing the door securely behind him. "Afraid you might be seen fraternizing with the enemy?"

"Yes. The last thing either of us needs just now is for one of my parents to show up. My mother has enough to deal with, and my father would jump to the wrong conclusions. He has rather old-fashioned ideas, one of them being that unmarried female guests do not entertain men in their rooms, at least not when they're staying under his roof."

"That must have cramped your style over the years. No wonder you were so fond of the cabana on the beach."

If he hadn't known he'd only make matters worse, he'd have laughed at the picture she made. She stood there defiant as a child, hurling insults at him in an effort to stave off another onslaught of tears. She held a wad of sodden tissues balled in her hand, her eyes were all puffy and pink, and her dainty little toes peeped out from beneath the hem of a white embroidered nightgown she'd surely inherited from some oversize Victorian ancestor.

"Caroline," he said mildly, careful not to betray so much as a smile, "I am not your enemy, nor do I consider you to be mine. This evening, I asked you to marry me, and I'm not here to tell you I've changed my mind. Rather, I hope that you now see the wisdom of accepting my proposal."

"Actually I don't," she hiccuped, her words interspersed with a volley of ragged sobs. "Gina hates me, and so does Clemente. They'll hate you, too, if you make me their stepmother."

"But I cannot take care of them alone, *cara.* I need your help, and whether or not you believe it, so do they."

"They need their mommy," she insisted, an observation he'd have thought was plain enough for anyone to see, but which, for some reason, brought about an even more violent outburst of tears from her. Turning away from him, she retreated to the bed, collapsed in a heap on the rumpled covers, and buried her face in her hands.

He made a fatal mistake, then. Moved beyond words, he went to her. Lowered himself next to her on the mattress. And unwisely chose to cradle her in his arms.

Her tears splashed warm and salty against his neck, leaving his shirt collar damp. Her hair teased his senses with the fragrance of sweet-smelling shampoo. Her slender frame shook uncontrollably against his chest. And he was lost, all his honorable intentions to give her space and time to consider his marriage proposal, reduced to smoldering dust.

She was a woman in need of a man. And he was not a man to turn away from a woman in need—especially not when her name was Caroline Leighton.

CHAPTER SIX

SHE could have tolerated anything else Paolo threw at her—mockery, scorn, disgust—used it to bolster her battered spirit, and thrown it back at him in kind. But his humanity completed the crushing despair Gina had begun with her rejection.

To Caroline's acute embarrassment, she found herself sobbing with the abandonment of a child. Past the point of caring how he might view such weakness, she collapsed in his arms and let go.

The floodgates opened. The tears flowed without end, accompanied by convulsive, almost primitive gasps of animal pain. Throughout, he said not a word. Instead he anchored her to him, and waited patiently for the storm to pass.

Just as well. Her senses were numbed to anything but the terrible morass of misery threatening to engulf her. Without his solid strength, she'd have descended too far into hell ever to find her way out again.

At last, though, the spate of tears slowed to a dribble, with only an occasional hiccup to fill the silence. Weak as a newborn lamb, she sagged against him.

His shirt was soaked, but he didn't seem to mind. Beneath the soggy fabric, his heartbeat, tireless and invincible, marked the passing seconds, its driving energy hers to use for however long she might need it. In a world gone increasingly crazy, he alone offered the haven she craved.

Eventually he said, “Feeling better, Caroline?”

Sounding like a woman with a serious adenoidal condition, she sniffled, “I suppose. It’s just so hard to accept that Gina wouldn’t turn to me for comfort. I *understand* it, up here.” She rapped her knuckles against her aching head. “I’m practically a stranger to her, after all. But my heart can’t seem to get the message.”

He stroked her hair; long, sweeping caresses of the kind a man might employ to soothe a frightened mare. “You do know you overreacted to her just now, don’t you? That this is about more than just the children?”

“Yes,” she admitted, perilously close to being swept under by another tidal wave of self-pity. “Every time I think I’ve accepted Vanessa’s death, it jumps up and bites me in the face all over again, and the least little thing sets me off. I’m an emotional wreck.”

“You’re allowed to be. We all are. Just because we’ve paid our last respects to those we love, doesn’t mean we’re over losing them.”

“But it’s not good for the children to see adults unable to cope. It frightens them.”

“Exactly. They need a return to stability.” His hand stilled briefly, and when he spoke again, his voice was laden with a huskiness she couldn’t quite decipher. “They need us in harmony, *cara mia.*”

She was beginning to think *she* needed *him,* far more than she’d ever have guessed. For reasons that defied logic, the man who’d once torn her life to pieces seemed to be the only one who could make her feel whole again. “Do you really believe we can make a go of marriage, Paolo?”

“Yes,” he answered, without a second’s hesitation. “I absolutely do.”

Trying to maintain a thread of common sense, she argued, "But apart from our both being committed to the children, what else do we have in common?"

He drew his hand down her face and cupped her cheek in his long, elegant fingers. "How about the fact that I find myself wanting more and more to stand between you and anyone who tries to hurt you, my lovely lady? That when I see you cry, I want to take your sadness and turn it to laugher? And if those are not reasons enough to convince you, then what if I tell you that, despite everything that has gone before, I trust you and want very much for you to know that you can trust me."

"Trust takes times, Paolo," she countered. "Like respect, it's something that has to be earned." *And as long as I keep the secret of the twins' paternity from you, I deserve neither your trust nor your respect....*

"Some things a man has to take on faith, Caroline," he said, his dark, beautiful eyes scouring her face.

Her heart pinched in guilty pain. "And you believe it's worth it, to give up your single life for a woman you barely know?" she asked, struggling to turn a deaf ear on her conscience. She had to be sure, before she told him, she reasoned. Spilling out the truth prematurely could hurt their chances of making the marriage work for reasons other than convenience.

He'd suggested a trial period of one year, but she was still looking for a happy ending to last a lifetime. Crazy though she might be, she'd fallen in love with him nine years ago, and realized she loved him still. All that foolish business to do with her legal rights to the children—what had that been about, really, but a desperate attempt to defend herself against his hurting her again?

She had come prepared for a battle that had never taken place, she realized, and that she'd entertained, even for a minute, the idea of using the children as a weapon, left her sick with self-disgust.

His mouth curled in a faint smile. "If you're asking me, will I be faithful, I give you my word it will be so. The reason I've not taken a wife sooner is that I was not willing to make a promise before God that I knew I couldn't keep."

Although it hurt to say the words, the question begged to be asked. "Yet you are now, with a woman you've admitted you don't love?"

"Yes," he said, with a candor that dealt a savage blow to her romantic fantasies. "Much has changed recently. Tragedy has struck and turned us all, particularly you and me, in a new direction. Suddenly we have children to consider. They must be our first priority. That much we owe them."

"And what of the rest?" Common sense told her not to press the point, but she couldn't help herself. "By themselves, children aren't enough to hold a marriage together, and I ought to know. Despite having two young daughters and a wife who needed him, my father walked out on my mother and left her to bring up Vanessa and me on her own."

"Then your father amounted to less than a man. To sire two children, then abandon both them and their mother is despicable."

He took stock of her again. "Listen to me, Caroline, and believe me when I tell you, I will not desert you."

"Then why bother to include the option to dissolve the marriage after one year?"

"Because I hoped it would make you feel less coerced. I am not so blinded by duty that I expect you to remain in a union you find intolerable. But let me make this much clear: if our marriage doesn't last, it will be because you decide to end it." His voice dropped suggestively. "And I intend to make it very difficult for you to arrive at such a choice."

If the way his arm tightened around her shoulders hadn't

warned her of his next move, the sexy, smoky note in his threat did. Starting with her forehead, he skimmed his mouth from her eyes to her jaw in a string of kisses that ended at her lips.

Such a mouth should be against the law, she thought, all the reasons she should call a halt to his behavior evaporating. If, in the course of their marriage, he never did more than simply kiss her, she could die a happy woman.

But he was bent on more erotic pleasure. With a low murmur of approval, he eased her down on the bed—not that he had to expend much energy to do that; already, she was limp with pleasure. Then, with the unhurried expertise of a man who'd had much practice, he unfastened the row of small pearl buttons running down the front of her nightgown, and parted the fabric to lay bare her breasts.

Still not satisfied, he continued dispensing with the garment. It yielded to his efforts, sliding down her torso in a soft sigh of surrender until it puddled around her waist. Another tug, and he had it past her hips and down her legs until not an inch of her was spared his inspection.

She had carried his two children practically full-term, and although her body had weathered the experience far better than most, the signs were there, if he cared to look for them. Plagued by a belated attack of nervous modesty, she tried to curl away from his gaze. But to no avail. Shaking his head in reproof, he manacled her wrists in the tender steel of one hand and imprisoned them above her head.

Helpless as a butterfly pinned to a collector's mat, she gave up the struggle and submitted to his absorbed scrutiny. His breath sifted over her, warm and light as a summer breeze.

"*Magnifica...incredibile...!*" he whispered, his sultry gaze scorching her flesh. "*Venero, la mia bella!*"

She'd studied enough Italian to know what his murmured words meant, but even if she'd been unfamiliar with the language, she'd have guessed that he liked what he saw. Only when his emotions ran high, be it from anger or, as now, from passion, did he lapse into his mother tongue with her.

What seduced her completely, though, was not that he eventually stopped looking and put his mouth everywhere on her, but that he did so with the reverence of a connoisseur examining a rare, exquisite work of art. Touches so fleeting they caressed her like a benediction.

Had he shown her the same tenderness the first time he'd seduced her, she'd probably have thought the melting delight he induced now was reward enough for giving him her virginity. But he'd taught her too well. She knew this was but a preface to much more explosive pleasure, and so did her body. The faint humming along her nerve endings, growing in volume until they buzzed, was evidence enough of that.

"Paolo…!" she sighed, squirming to free her hands from his grip. "Let me touch you…."

"Patience, my lovely," he breathed in Italian, settling his mouth again at her throat. "We have all night to enjoy one another."

"Not if your father finds you here."

She wished she hadn't reminded him. Abandoning her without a second's hesitation, he rose from the bed and strode to the door. "Indeed not. He would awaken the entire household with his outrage."

Regret leached away all the lovely anticipation building in her blood, and left her aching with disappointment. No point trying to delude herself that she'd feel differently in the morning and be glad she'd called a halt to things. She wanted him with a deep and vital yearning that had its roots in something far more enduring than the temporary release of good sex. She wanted to belong to him in every way that counted: physically, emotionally, spiritually.

She'd grown up without a father, or uncles or brothers. Of course, she had a son, as well as a daughter, but even for them, she had Paolo to thank. At the end of the day, he was the *only* man ever to have left an indelible impression on her soul.

At last accepting that it was something that neither time nor circumstance would ever change, she tossed aside the last of her pride and begged, "Paolo, please don't go!"

"I must," he said roughly, and before she could repeat her plea, the door had closed behind him.

Desolated, she gathered a fistful of sheet, and crushed it against her mouth to silence the wave of anguish threatening to erupt. To have come so close to heaven, and then, with a few ill-chosen words, to lose it all, was beyond cruel. It was inhumane, torture of the worst kind, and she wanted to howl at the unfairness of a world which would allow such suffering.

Then, miraculously, the door opened again, and Paolo was there again. Stunned, delighted, *grateful,* she said, "I thought you'd left and weren't coming back."

"Not coming back?" Locking her door, he tossed the key on the nearby dresser, and began to remove his clothes. "Caroline, my angel, I couldn't stay away, even if I wanted to."

By the time he reached the bed again, he was as naked as she was. And, like her, he'd changed over the years. The younger playboy son of the almighty Salvatore Rainero had matured into a man of impressive stature, and she was mesmerized by the magnificence of him.

He'd always been classically tall, dark and handsome, but at twenty-four there'd been a hint of softness in his build, an indication of too much fast living, coupled with a distinct lack of self-discipline. He'd worn too much jewelry. A heavy gold chain hung around his neck. Diamonds rimmed the dial of his gold watch. Another diamond graced the signet ring on his little finger. Smitten though she'd been at the time, she'd found such a conspicuous display of wealth somewhat tasteless.

Now, he wore only a slim gold watch which he discarded along with his clothes, and a simple chain that glimmered softly against his deep olive skin. His chest had deepened, his shoulders broadened with muscle more cleanly defined than before. His limbs were strong, his flanks lean, his belly flat and hard. And his masculinity…?

"Will I do?" he asked, standing close enough for her to reach out and touch him.

Heavenly days, but he was fearsomely endowed, impressively aroused! "I think you'll do very well indeed," she managed to say, drawing her legs under her until she knelt before him, "and not just for tonight."

"What are you saying, Caroline?"

She drew in a tortured breath, and ran her tongue over her lips. "*Yes.* I'm saying, *yes,* I *will* marry you."

A light flared in his dark eyes, a mixture of triumph and relief. "Then let me say this. Look at me now and see that I am far from perfect. Know that I will make mistakes, and there will be times when I might do or say things that make you wish you'd never agreed to become my wife."

Lowering himself next to her, he pinned her in that forthright stare which had become so much his trademark, and continued, "It would be very easy for me to tell you that I love you, Caroline. But they are not words to be spoken lightly, and although you and I go back a long way, we have spent but a few days in each other's company. So I will save such a declaration for a later time, when they will carry true meaning, and for now say instead, without reservation, that I admire you, and I desire you."

He took her hand and placed it flat against his chest. "With every beat of this heart, I promise I will never deliberately cause you pain. I will never lie to you, and I will never betray our married covenant. Your honesty and gentleness…they inspire me, *tesoro,* and give me hope for the future."

This time, conscience clamored to be heard, deafening her with pleas to come clean. This beautiful man was offering himself to her just as he was, unembellished by any false declarations brought on by spur-of-the-moment euphoria, but with a sincere, straightforward commitment to be the best that he could be, as her partner, as her husband.

And what had she to give him in return? A secret grown so burdensome that she didn't know how to divulge it without ruining everything. She'd let chance after chance pass her by, because she'd believed hoarding the truth about the children was her only weapon against the man she'd viewed for so long as her enemy. Now, her silence stood to rob her of her most powerful ally.

One way or another, she had to tell him the truth—and soon. To wait to do so until they were husband and wife would strike at the very foundation of what their marriage was all about.

Do it now! her conscience urged. *Tell him, and beg his forgiveness for waiting so long! It's not too late. Together you can make this work. He's not the same man anymore. He'll understand. See how he's looking at you…feel the tenderness in his touch. Do it now, before you lose your nerve.*

"Paolo," she began, her voice quivering with apprehension, "I'm not exactly perfect myself. There are…things about me that you don't know about. Secrets you deserve to—"

"I long since guessed as much, Caroline," he said, stopping her with a finger to her lips, "but nothing you have to tell me will change the fact that you are a good woman who will make a fine surrogate mother to Clemente and Gina. And isn't that what our marriage is really all about?"

"Yes, but—"

"No 'buts.'" He drew her hand down his chest until it nested against his groin. "We sit here naked beside each other, on a bed large enough to hold both of us and impatient passion yearning to be fulfilled, yet we squander our time with talking? No, *la mia bella,* the talking can wait for another day."

His erection had diminished somewhat, but at her touch,

it sprang up with renewed vigor. Hot, silken, urgent, it throbbed against her palm, and no amount of guilty conscience could hold her back from cradling him possessively.

"Yes," he whispered, cupping her breasts and lowering his head to adore them with his mouth and his tongue. "Just so do we forge the bonds that will unite us."

How could she disagree, when her blood surged with excitement, and her heart cartwheeled madly behind her ribs? How pretend she was unmoved by his attention, when his tongue dipped lower and slipped between the folds of her flesh to find her wet with need? And how in the world silence her smothered, frantic exclamations as the climax she'd denied herself for so long swept over her in a storm so violent that she almost screamed?

I love you...I love you...!

The words rang in her head, fighting to be aired aloud. "I want you," she begged instead. "Paolo, I want you now, inside me...*please!*"

He reached for a small foil packet he'd tossed on the dresser, along with the door key, and the reason he'd briefly left the room finally hit home. "Give me a moment," he replied, his chest heaving. "We have enough to cope with. Let's not muddy the waters with a pregnancy neither of us wants or needs. If we remain married, it has to be from choice, not obligation."

Too late, she thought, the ecstasy he'd so easily induced evaporating in the dismal knowledge that he'd just made confession that much more difficult for her to accomplish.

He put on the contraceptive. Then, oblivious to the real reason he'd cast a cloud on the moment, took her in his arms again. "You look downcast, my lovely. Do you not agree that for us to make a baby would be unfair, both to the child, and to the twins?"

"Of course," she managed.

She must not have sounded convincing enough because he reared back, the better to search her face. "Yet you remain downcast. You surely don't believe a condom spoils the pleasure either of us gives to the other?"

"No," she said miserably.

"Then what?"

"I just want you to make love to me. You said we shouldn't waste the night in talk, yet that's what we seem to be doing."

"Worry not, Caroline," he murmured, his hands molding her to him, "the night is still very young. We have hours to spend together, and I have come prepared to make use of every one."

He did stop talking then, and devoted himself to confirming what she'd known for years: that all it took to bring her senses to sizzling life was the right man.

No hurried, impatient seduction this time, but a leisurely, erotic tour of her body conducted with minute attention to every curve, every indentation, every smooth, bare stretch of skin. His eyes, heavy-lidded with barely leashed passion, blazed a trail of heat from her head to her toes. His hands shaped her every contour with the tactile dedication of a blind man. His mouth and tongue left a wicked, heavenly trail of discovery from the outer shell of her ear to the high arch of her instep; from her throat to the back of her knees.

And yet, although with every touch, he stoked her to fever pitch, not once did he trespass between her thighs to the cloistered fold of flesh screaming for his possession. He knew how to tantalize, to torment, until she was begging incoherently—garbled, frantic words of pleading known only to lovers dancing on the brink of destruction.

Beside herself, she dragged his mouth back to hers. Tasted on him the perfume of her body lotion, of herself. Slid her hands down his torso until she found him, pulsing slick and hard and hot within the condom—so close to losing control that the sweat gleamed on his forehead and left his lungs battered with the effort to withhold himself just a minute longer…another second. And in the end, as he'd always known he would, losing the battle.

With the deep, agonized groan of a man in agony, he plunged deep inside her. Held himself immobile, and clenched his jaw so hard, the veins stood out on his neck like ropes. A useless exercise, one he could never win. Because the demons of desire had too strong a hold—on him, on her.

Wrapping her legs around his waist, she imprisoned him and, for the first time since she'd conceived his children, she felt complete. Free to give, free to take, free to love with her whole heart and soul and body.

"Slowly, *tesoro,*" he whispered harshly, with a futile attempt to delay the inevitable.

But even if she'd been able to obey the plea, he could not. Driven by a hunger too long delayed, his own flesh betrayed him. He rocked against her, fiercely, urgently. Hypnotized by the consuming rhythm, she responded involuntarily and the storm prowling impatiently at the outer limits of her consciousness, let fly with the first distant roll of thunder.

A spasm clutched at her. Released her and retreated, to gather strength for its next onslaught. Clutched again, more tightly…and then again, this time so powerfully that she thought she might die.

Paolo stilled, tense as an overwound spring about to fly apart. "Ah, Caroline, *mia bella…mio amore!*" he muttered, dragging the words from the very depths of his being, then drove into her one last time, a deep, hard, hungry, merciless thrust.

It spelled the end, of order, of coherence, of life as she knew it. She dissolved, became nothing—a moonbeam caught in a spinning web of sensation. Sound filled her, rushing like the wind, lifting her. She heard a voice that once was hers crying out as sensation rippled over her, carried her forward implacably, and hurled her past the point of no return.

She toppled, would have fallen off the edge of the earth, spun off into eternity, had Paolo not held her fast. His body shuddered, groaned; a mighty ship fighting an impossible sea. He was drowning, and so was she. And it didn't matter, because they were together, welded limb to limb, body to body, heart to heart.

She surfaced a long time later, a new woman with a new life, in a new world, one composed of serene moonlight slanting through the windows to splash the dark purple shadows of her room with pale blue stripes. Paolo sprawled on top of her, spent and breathless. And she loved it. Loved the damp warmth of his breath against her neck, the exhausted weight of him.

Again, the words fought to escape. *I love you…I've loved you forever….*

He stirred, lifted his head and regarded her from passion-sated eyes. "I suppose I should go so that you can sleep in peace."

"No," she said, stroking his beautiful face. "You should stay. I want you to stay, Paolo. Don't ever leave me again."

"I hoped you'd say that," he said, a sleepy smile curving his mouth, and still buried inside her, he rolled to his side and drew her close again.

When she next became conscious of time, the moon had slipped beyond the house and left her room in total darkness. But she didn't need light to know that, in sleep, she and Paolo had lost their intimate connection. Now he lay with his leg flung over her, and the way his palm closed possessively over her breast told her he, too, was awake, and hungry for her all over again.

The sweet, lazy pace of their second loving stole her breath away. *This,* she thought, sinking her teeth into her lower lip as the pleasure built to a slow crescendo, *is how it will be between us from now on. Sometimes fast and furious, and sometimes so unbearably tender that it will make me cry.*

It won't matter if he can't say the words, because I'll feel his love, just as I do now. Then I'll be brave enough to tell him things I might not dare to say in the bright light of morning. Share secrets that won't seem so frightening under cover of night. Tell him the truth about the babies. And he'll forgive me, because he'll see that I did what I thought was best at the time.

The past won't matter anymore, because we'll have the future, and we'll have our children. We'll make up for lost time, and accept the way fate has brought us together again. Vanessa and Ermanno's deaths won't seem such a terrible waste, but, rather, part of God's greater, grander plan.

"Caroline," he whispered urgently, straining against her.

Inflamed by the passion in his voice, she replied, "I'm here," and contracted around him with a soft cry as his seed ran free.

CHAPTER SEVEN

HAD it not been for the perpetual shadow of Vanessa's and Ermanno's deaths, the next two weeks would have numbered among the happiest of Callie's life. In line with Paolo's wishes, everyone stayed the extra two weeks on the island, although she'd have preferred it to be just he, she, and the children, seeing it as the ideal chance to meld them into a foursome without any outside interference.

But, mindful of too many changes at once, Paolo asked his parents to stay behind, too. "Maintaining a sense of continuity with the familiar," he reasoned, "will help the twins accept their new living arrangements more readily."

His insight and obvious deep concern for them warmed Callie's heart. How could she help but adore him, when he gave so much of himself to children he didn't even know were really his? Coupled with her own love for them, it could only strengthen the odds in favor of the marriage.

She also suspected Paolo had spoken with his father; perhaps gone so far as to warn him to curb his hostility, because Salvatore grew, if not all warm and fuzzy toward her, at least not as openly antagonistic.

"It is good to see you getting along better with our grandchildren," he decreed at breakfast, a few days after she'd accepted Paolo's proposal. "I believe they begin to feel some affection for you."

Oh, she hoped so—she thought so! Certainly, they'd shown themselves more willing to include her in their activities. "Will you come, too, Zia Caroline?" Clemente wanted to know, the afternoon Paolo suggested a sunset cruise in the thirty-nine-foot luxury cruiser moored in the protected marina below the villa.

"Of course," she told him, and had to blink back a rush of tears at the smile that lit up his face.

Her baby boy…her son! Strong and handsome as his father, but with a gentleness that reminded Callie of Lidia, and of her own mother. How proud Audrey Leighton would have been, of both her grandchildren.

Another day, Gina decided the time was ripe for a game of hide-and-seek. "Zia Caroline and I will play against you and Clemente," she ordered her uncle, shepherding everyone outside to an iron gate overlooking a formal garden in the grand Italian style, "and you will not cheat."

"If you say so," Paolo replied meekly, which made Callie smile.

Gina was definitely her father's child, strong-willed, forthright, and independent. She made up her own mind about things, regardless of outside influence. "I didn't much like you at first, even though Nonna said I must," she'd announced bluntly the previous evening, while she allowed Callie to braid her hair, "but you're actually quite nice now that I've got to know you better. I wouldn't mind if you stayed with us forever. It's not as good as when Mommy was here, of course, but it's nice to have someone who knows how to do my hair. Nonna isn't very good at it, and when Zio Paolo once tried, he made a terrible mess of it."

"We'll hide first," she decided now, directing her brother and Paolo to cover their eyes and count to a hundred. Then taking Callie's hand, she ran with her along a crushed gravel path lined with marble statuary. "Follow me, Zia," she said. "I know exactly the place to hide."

Skirting a pond filled with lily pads floating around an elaborate stone fountain, she ducked between two stone benches and through an opening carved in a hedge. "Behind this," she whispered, pulling aside a trailing vine to reveal a natural grotto filled with ferns. "They'll never find us here. This is my secret place. I've never shown it to Clemente. Only Mommy knows about it…." Her voice wavered briefly. "And now you."

"I'm very honored that you'd share it with me," Callie said thickly, hearing the sudden desolation in the child's voice, and desperately wanting to comfort her. But she knew well enough that Gina wouldn't welcome a display of affection she hadn't initiated herself.

"You won't tell anyone else, will you, Zia Caroline?"

"No," she promised. "Nor will I ever come here unless you invite me."

Sighing, Gina wandered deeper into the grotto. "Mommy and I used to light candles sometimes," she said, suddenly despondent. "Up there, see, in those little glass jars. Then we'd sit on cushions we brought from the house, and talk about private things that boys and fathers don't understand. But I don't think the candles would be a good idea today."

"No," Callie said softly. "That's something special that belonged just to you and your mommy. Also, we don't want to give ourselves away, and there's enough light filtering through from outside that we can see quite well."

In fact, in the dim green light and with the vine swinging gently in the breeze, sending waves of shadow rippling over the sandy floor, the effect was a little like being in an underwater cave.

Suddenly Gina tipped her head to one side, listening intently, then pressed a finger to her lips, her mood brightening. "I can hear them coming," she whispered. "Let's hide at the very back. We can sit on the rocks."

It was darker there, and much cooler. Enough that Callie shivered and wished she'd worn a jacket over her light sweater. Gina must have felt the chill, too, because without waiting to be invited, she curled up close beside her.

Callie held her breath, ever so casually draped her arm around her daughter's shoulders, and braced herself for a rejection that never came. Instead, to her indescribable pleasure, Gina snuggled closer and said, "You feel nice and warm, Zia…just the way Mommy used to."

Approaching footsteps ruled out the possibility of a verbal reply, and just as well. The aching lump in her throat would have prevented Callie from doing more than choke on any attempt at a response. Instead, she acknowledged the enormous compliment by tucking Gina more securely in the curve of her arm.

"They couldn't have come this far," Paolo said, from immediately outside the entrance to the cave. An inch closer, and he'd have stepped past the vine and found them. "There's nothing here but a path to the beach, and we'd see them if they'd gone there."

"Gina often comes this way. I've watched her, and even followed her once, but I lost her. Sometimes, she's almost too smart for me," Clemente said, an admission that left Gina snorting on a giggle.

Paolo cleared his throat, rather loudly, Callie thought. "We'd better double back, then. They might have run behind the hedge and are already waiting at the gate. If they're not, we'll look in the atrium. There are all kinds of places they could hide in there."

Their voices faded as they hiked back toward the villa. "Boys are *so* easy to fool," Gina crowed, once silence descended again. "They're not a bit like us, are they, Zia Caroline?"

"No," she said, tearful emotion still swirling dangerously close to the surface. To hold her daughter like this, to share confidences, and private jokes, were gifts beyond price, and she wouldn't have traded them for all the riches in the world. "Should we make a run for the gate now, do you think?"

Gina shook her head. "I quite like just sitting here with you," she said shyly, and just like that added the touch of perfection to an already extraordinary day.

Later, over predinner drinks, Paolo cornered Callie, and under cover of the general buzz of conversation, murmured, "Did you enjoy hiding out with your niece in the grotto?"

She laughed, taken aback. "You guessed we were there?"

"Of course I guessed! Even if I didn't know this island like the back of my hand, I'd have been hard-pressed not to hear the tittering filtering through that convenient screen of shrubbery."

"Then why didn't you call us on it?"

Warming her to the core with his slow smile, he said, "The two of you seemed to be bonding. I decided it was best not to disturb you."

Flustered at the way his gaze lingered on her, she averted her eyes and said, "You do that rather often lately, you know. Your parents will begin to notice."

"Do what?"

"Smile at me, look at me, as if we're up to something wicked."

"But we are, Caroline. We're secretly engaged."

"The way you're behaving, it won't be a secret much longer."

She wasn't exaggerating. He frequently locked glances with her—across the dinner table, or while they were taking morning coffee with his parents in the solarium, or during an evening game of chess between him and his father—and the look in his eyes, the curve of his mouth, would send the heat rushing to her face. They were the smiles, the glances, a lover bestowed on his lady—the kind that said he couldn't wait to undress her.

And it seemed that he couldn't. Every night without fail, after the rest of the household slept, he'd come to her. She'd lie in her bed, her body naked beneath the sheet and trembling with expectation. The door would open, and she'd see his silhouette outlined briefly against the night light shining in the upstairs hall before he stepped, silent as a shadow, into the room. A second later, the lock would snick softly in place, and he'd cross to the bed.

She'd rise up on the mattress to meet him, and they'd come together in a flurry of eager hands, and hungry lips, and labored breathing. He'd kiss her all over, bring her to orgasm with his finger, his tongue. Then, while she was still shimmering with ecstasy and he was thick and heavy with desire, he'd plunge inside her, and rock so urgently that she sometimes wondered how the condom he always used didn't split apart.

Oh, yes! Regardless of whatever else might occur during the day, she could always count on the nights!

"Let's take a walk on the beach," he suggested, catching her as she finished lunch, toward the end of the second week. "We need to talk."

Overhearing, the twins chimed in. "Us, too, Zio Paolo?"

"Not this time," he said. "What I have to say to Caroline is private for now, but I promise to share the secret with you soon. In any case, you have to spend the afternoon catching up on your studies, otherwise when you go back to class, you'll find yourselves behind your school friends."

The minute they were out of earshot of the villa, Caroline asked, "Is there a problem?"

"Yes," he said, curbing a grin at the anxiety printed all over her face. "I've been thinking about what you said, the other day—about my parents figuring out what we're up to—and you're right. I don't seem able to stay out of your bed, and sooner or later, I'm going to get caught. Quite apart from the indignity of such an occurrence, I resent having to sneak around like a teenager."

"So what do you want to do about it?"

He clasped her hand and helped her over the low wall separating the gardens from the beach. "Announce our engagement and make it official."

Her fingers tightened around his. "Do you think the children are ready to hear it?"

"I think there's only one way to find out."

She chewed the corner of her mouth uneasily. "What about your parents?"

"I don't consider their reaction to be particularly relevant, *cara.* We did not reach this decision lightly, and hardly need their blessing."

"It would be nice to have it, though," she said wistfully. "It's been a long time since I really felt part of a family."

"You'll be a crucial part of the one we make together, Caroline. The children and I will be your family. And you must know my mother will welcome you as a daughter."

"It's not your mother I'm worried about."

This time he did laugh at the expression on her face, which reminded him of a child being forced to swallow bad-tasting medicine. "I'll deal with my father. He won't give you any trouble."

She kicked at the sand, sending it spraying up around her ankles. She had very nice ankles. Very nice everything. "When are you thinking of telling them?"

"Tonight, before dinner. I've instructed Jolanda to prepare something special. We'll toast to the future with champagne, although the children will have to make do with sparkling fruit juice."

"And you're absolutely sure you want to go through with the marriage?"

"Absolutely." Surprised at the note of apprehension in her voice, he slowed to a stop. "Aren't you?"

"Yes, Paolo," she said. "After the way things have been between me and the children this last while, I think I have a fighting chance of making it work with them."

"And with me?"

She lifted her shoulders in a faint shrug. "I want to make you happy."

"You already do, *cara mia.*"

"I do?"

"Why else do you think I can't keep out of your bed?"

Her blue eyes all at once alight with impish laughter, she said pertly, "Because you're afraid of the dark?" and danced away from him when he tried to grab hold of her.

Prompted by a burst of desire as fierce as it was unexpected, he chased her behind a jutting pillar of sandstone and caught her to him, reveling in the feel of her body, pressed warm and soft against his; in the scent of her hair, her skin.

The idea of claiming her as his wife now seemed to him as natural as breathing. Without knowing exactly when or how it had happened, she'd wormed her way so thoroughly into his heart that he couldn't imagine life without her.

Could it be that he, whom a previous mistress had tearfully dismissed as "unable to commit to anyone who wasn't family" had finally met his match? It seemed so to him, because if what he felt for Caroline didn't amount to love, then how else to describe the light that filled his spirit at the mention of her name, or whenever she walked into the room?

Unsure that she was ready to hear the words he longed to speak, he adopted a teasing tone and said, "Running away isn't acceptable, Caroline. Now that you've agreed to make our engagement public, you officially belong to me."

"Oh?" She lowered her lashes, flirting shamelessly with him. "Am I in trouble, then?"

"Most definitely. I shall have to devise some kind of punishment, to keep you in line."

"Will you accept this as an apology, instead?"

Without warning, she rose up on her toes and kissed his jaw, then ran her tongue down the open neck of his shirt to the base of his throat. The response which jerked through him, sending the blood rushing to his loins, was so powerful and instantaneous that he almost came.

Shaken that his control could be so suddenly and severely tested, he glanced back along the beach. Assured they were well out of sight of the villa, he spun around and bracing himself against the pillar of sandstone at his back, pinned her to him.

She wore a pleated skirt with a hem that just covered her knees. It took but a moment for him to lift it, and inch his finger inside the elasticized leg of her panties.

She was hot and swollen and wet. Already whimpering with need, and reaching for him.

Another moment and she had the fly of his blue jeans unsnapped. He sprang into her searching hand, fully erect and pulsing on the brink of explosion.

Heart thundering, fingers fumbling, he ground out, "Your underwear's in the way."

"Rip it, then," she panted, "but for God's sake, hurry up!"

Sliding his hands beneath her sweet, slender buttocks, he lifted her until her legs were twined around his waist. "This is craziness, *tesoro!* I don't have a condom with me."

"I don't care!"

Nor did she! Reaching down with her free hand, she tore at her cotton panties until she'd uncovered herself, and could guide him home. Her flesh welcomed him, hot and tight as a silk glove. He drove into her, filling her completely.

"Ahh!" Her head fell back, and she closed her eyes, the

first ripples of orgasm already taking hold. "Faster, Paolo… harder…deeper…!"

They could make a baby, and his conscience cared that he was taking such a risk. But his body belonged to her, and he could no more reclaim it than he could count the grains of sand beneath his feet. She possessed him without mercy, and when he came in a hot, shuddering burst, she clamped her legs more tightly around him and milked him of every last drop of seed.

Spent, he buckled at the knees, and taking her with him, sprawled on the beach in a tangle of limbs. Sand trickled over them, cool, impersonal, nonjudgmental. But he could not so easily exonerate himself.

Stroking the hair back from her face, he said, "You realize I could have impregnated you? That we could already have placed our marriage in jeopardy?"

"Because of a baby?" Her eyes stared back at him unfocused, still glazed with the residue of passion. "How could an innocent baby possibly do that?"

"By placing an impossible strain on all of us. Already, we are stand-in parents to two children in need of security. They should not have to compete with a third who is our own blood child."

Her gaze flickered, slid away from his. "They wouldn't have to, if we made them feel just as loved," she said, feverishly attempting to restore order to her clothing—a hopeless task where her underwear was concerned, but she seemed determined to try to repair it. Seemed determined to do anything, however hopeless, rather than acknowledge his very real concerns.

Catching her hands, he forced them to be still. "Look at me, Caroline, and stop trying to fix something as insignificant as a pair of cotton underpants, when we have bigger problems facing us. You say we'd love our niece and nephew as much as a child of our own, but how can you guarantee that would be the case? Think of it, *cara!* A baby you carried in your womb for nine months which, once it was born, would demand all your attention. How could you possibly divide yourself fairly among three, when your heart truly belonged to only one?"

"How could I not?" she whispered, her eyes swimming in sudden, inexplicable tears. "Gina and Clemente are my own…sister's children."

He could have kicked himself. Vanessa's death was never far from her thoughts, and all he'd accomplished by airing his concerns was remind her of her recent loss. "Forgive me," he said contritely. "I didn't mean to make you cry, nor do I blame you for my carelessness."

"You should," she replied, her mouth trembling uncontrollably. "I'm the one who insisted we make love."

Smiling despite himself, he said, "In case you haven't noticed, *cara mia,* no woman can seduce a man unless he's willing! Protecting you from an unplanned pregnancy is my responsibility, and I let you down."

"Well, you're probably worrying for nothing," she said, pulling herself together a little. "It's the wrong time of the month for me to conceive."

"But we can't rely on that as a foolproof method of contraception," he pointed out gently.

"What are you suggesting, then? That if I'm pregnant, I sneak back to Rome and find a back-street abortionist?"

"*Dio,* no!" he exclaimed, shocked almost speechless. "Caroline, *tesoro,* I would never permit you to have an abortion. All I'm saying is that, in view of what happened between us this afternoon, making a formal announcement of our engagement has become that much more imperative. Should it turn out that you are, in fact, pregnant, a wedding arranged to take place quickly would eliminate any suggestion that we married for the sake of an unborn child. It's the least we can do for the twins, to let them be assured they're not an afterthought in the arrangement."

Subdued, and seeming still too embarrassed to look him in the face, she sifted sand between her fingers and mumbled, "Oh...yes...I see your point."

"Then we're agreed. We'll move forward without delay. Will two weeks give you enough time to prepare?"

"More than enough," she said, at last meeting his gaze. "We're in mourning, Paolo. A big wedding would be inappropriate."

"It doesn't have to be a grand affair, to be memorable. But if I have my way, this will be your *only* shot at being a bride, and you deserve something more than a brief ceremony crammed in between the many other things we have to do in order to set up house together. One thing at a time, however." He climbed to his feet, put his own clothing to rights, then extended a hand to her. "Come along, my love. Let's return to the house and prepare for an eventful evening ahead. Wedding details can wait until after we've broken the news to the family."

"Engaged?"

Paolo's announcement, delivered during the cocktail hour, brought the entire room to a standstill. Lidia's mouth fell open and she clasped her hands at her breast, a ray of pure joy lighting her face for the first time since the funerals. The children merely looked mystified, but were sufficiently impressed by the sudden electricity charging the atmosphere to stop bickering over the puzzle they were working on, and slink closer to each other on the sofa.

Poor lambs, Callie thought, watching them. They'd learned at far too young an age that life could deal some vicious blows on the innocent, and were obviously afraid another was in the offing.

Salvatore, however, the only one who'd responded verbally to the news, and not very agreeably at that, said again, with more emphasis this time, as if Paolo had spoken in foreign tongues, "*Engaged?* To Caroline?"

"That's right," Paolo said. "I proposed to her, and she accepted. Congratulate me, Father."

Salvatore scowled and favored her with a look loaded with such suspicion that Callie half-expected him to accuse her of entrapment. "When did all this take place?"

"Several days ago."

"And you wait until now, to spring the news on us?"

"Caroline needed some time to decide if she wanted me for a husband." Paolo smiled at her over the rim of his aperitif glass. "I'm very happy to say that, after due consideration, she decided she does."

Clemente spoke up, his brow furrowed in confusion. "How can you and Zia Caroline get married? Uncles shouldn't marry aunts."

"Especially not in this case," his grandfather muttered in an aside.

Shooting his father a quelling glare, Paolo explained, "They can if they're not related to one another, Clemente."

"I don't understand how."

"Well, when you're grown up, you and Gina might be aunt and uncle to each other's children, but you could never marry her because she's your sister and you're her brother."

Clemente digested that information quickly enough. "I wouldn't marry her even if I could," he declared. "She's too bossy!"

Ignoring him, Gina appealed to Paolo, her little face anxious. "Does that mean you're going to live in America with her, Zio?"

"No. We plan to live in Rome, quite near your old house."

"Oh, this is wonderful!" Lidia exclaimed, setting down her vermouth and embracing first Callie, then Paolo. "The best news in the world! When is the wedding to be?"

"As soon as you and Caroline can put one together," he said. "Preferably within the next two or three weeks."

"So soon? Paolo, a wedding takes time to arrange."

"Not this one," Callie interjected. "We want something small and private."

"What's the big rush?" Salvatore asked, his radar still obviously on high alert. "We are a family in mourning."

"Which is exactly why we want to keep the fuss to a minimum." Paolo turned to the twins. "But there's more. Zia Caroline and I would like to make a home for the two of you. We want you to come and live with us."

"So that's what this is really all about!" Salvatore blew out a breath of undisguised relief. "I was beginning to think you'd taken leave of your senses."

Paolo fixed him in a severe look. "If you cannot be happy for Caroline and me, Father, then at least have the good grace to keep quiet."

By then oblivious to the mounting tension, Gina bounced up and down on the sofa in excitement. "Can I be a bridesmaid? My friend Anita was a bridesmaid when her uncle got married, and she wore a pretty dress, with flowers in her hair."

Callie was about to say no, it wasn't going to be that kind of wedding, but Paolo spoke up first. "Of course you may. Every bride should have a maid to help her on her wedding day, just as every groom should have a best man." He eyed his nephew. "Are you willing to take on the job, Clemente, or do I ask someone else to do it?"

"I'll do it," Clemente said solemnly, "but first I have a question. Everything you say makes Gina and me feel happy, Zio Paolo, but how can that be right when our parents just died?"

Callie's heart constricted. "Oh, honey," she said softly, drawing him to her, "don't ever feel you don't have the right to be happy. Your mommy and daddy wouldn't want that, at all."

"But won't they think we'll forget them, if we come to live with you?"

"No," she assured him. "Because they know we'll never be able to take their place. We're just standing in for them."

"Will they know we'll still miss them?"

How sensitive he was, this young son of hers. Moved, she said, "Of course they will. We'll all miss them. But I think they'll feel better knowing your uncle and I are there to look after you."

"They have their grandmother and me," Salvatore reminded her sourly.

"Yes." She spared him a passing glance. "But even you must agree that children can never have too many people who care about them, and whether or not you believe it, Signor Rainero, your grandchildren's welfare is something I hold very dear to my heart."

If he wasn't impressed by her remarks, Clemente was. His mouth curving in a tiny smile, he said, "You're nice, Zia Caroline."

"Nice enough to be given a hug?"

He screwed up his face, debating the question. "Okay," he said finally, and came into her embrace.

It was the first time she'd ever felt his arms close around her as if he meant it, instead of as if it was a duty he was compelled to perform. Struggling to hang on to her composure, she looked to Paolo for help.

"Enough of trying to strangle my future wife, young man," he decreed, all mock indignation mixed with laughter. "And no tears from you, Caroline, or you, Momma! Tonight is for celebrating."

"So that's why there's champagne chilling," Salvatore said, drumming up a token smile. "Well, since you've both made up your minds, I suppose I should propose a toast."

CHAPTER EIGHT

DINNER that night was almost festive. *Almost.*

"We'll have to find a dress for your big day, Caroline, and also one for Gina," Lidia said. "I would so love to go shopping with you and introduce you to my favorite designer."

"You're welcome to come shopping with me, but I hadn't thought of buying anything too extravagant," Callie said, only to be shot down, surprisingly, by Salvatore.

"If you're worried about money," he pronounced bluntly, between sips of the very excellent champagne served with the meal, "do not be. A suitable wedding outfit will be our gift to you."

Was he deliberately condescending to her, as if he feared she might appear at the altar wearing red sequins and feathers, Callie wondered, bristling, or was this his heavy-handed way of welcoming her into the family?

"That's very generous of you, Signor Rainero," she replied coolly, "but it's not the money I'm concerned about. I'm well able to buy my own dress, and Gina's, too. But the kind of wedding Paolo and I want doesn't call for a designer gown. I'm certain I can find something *suitable* in any good department store, of which I'm sure there are many in Rome."

Ever mindful of his aristocratic heritage, Salvatore covered his contempt at such a suggestion with a strenuously benign smile—the kind, Callie was willing to bet, that would leave his face aching for the next half hour. "My dear lady, the Raineros do not shop in department stores! You'll find plenty of other opportunities to wear a designer gown, once the wedding is a fait accompli."

He paused, long enough to take another sip of champagne and fastidiously dab his linen napkin to the corner of his mouth, then concluded, "Indeed, one such item of haute couture will not begin to fill your needs. As my son's wife, you will attend many formal functions, and frequently find your photograph dominating the society pages of Italian newspapers, not to mention the more respectable international magazines. You might as well accept that fact, and start out the way you'll be obliged to carry on."

At her side, Paolo stiffened and covered her suddenly clenched fist warmly with his hand. "Caroline's role as my wife is something she and I will determine together, Father, without input from you, or anyone else," he said evenly.

"I'm interfering, am I?" Salvatore's amusement showed a singular lack of remorse. "Very well, I'll keep my opinions to myself, provided you allow me one concession." He directed another too-amiable smile Callie's way, this one even more fixed than its predecessor. "That, as the newest member of my family, Caroline, you call me Suocero, which in Italian means—"

"Father-in-law," she finished for him. "Yes, Signor Rainero, I'm aware of that. I took several university courses in Italian, and am quite fluent in the language."

He regarded her with sly triumph, as if he'd just caught her red-handed in a lie. "I don't understand. Didn't you say you studied architecture?"

"That is correct."

"Then why such an interest in learning Italian?"

Because I wanted to be able to communicate with my children, in the event that they didn't learn English.

"The influence of the Italian Renaissance and Baroque period on modern architecture is huge. I spent one summer session studying in Florence, Milan and Venice. A working knowledge of the language was essential."

"One summer, hmm." Continuing to regard her narrowly, he plucked at his lower lip with one finger. "Was that the same year you visited your sister and her children?"

"Yes. At the end of the semester, I came to Rome and spent a few days with Vanessa and her family."

"They were an afterthought, were they?"

"Hardly!"

"I don't remember you coming to see us," Gina chimed in.

Silently blessing the child for causing a distraction before she lost her temper with the mistrustful old fool destined to be her father-in-law, Callie explained, "That's because you were very little then, Gina. Still babies, really, not even two years old. You probably only remember coming to see me in San Francisco, when you were older."

Clemente nodded enthusiastically. "I remember doing that! You live in a town house, at the top of a hill, and you have a fireplace in your salon, and if you stand at the window and look down the hill, you can see an island with an old prison on it."

"That's right," she said, pathetically grateful that he'd kept a little part of her life locked away in his memory. "It's called Alcatraz. I'll take you to visit it some time, if you like."

"How can you do that? It's a long way away, and I don't want to live in America." Gina turned accusing eyes on her uncle. "You said we're going to live here, Zio Paolo."

"We are," he said soothingly. "But we might take a holiday in San Francisco, once in a while. You wouldn't mind that, would you?"

"Not as long as I don't have to stay there. I'd miss Nonna and Nonno, and all my friends."

"Just as we'd miss you," her grandfather said, his glance again settling on Callie with brief and telling intent. "Far too much to allow you to live so far away."

Allow? she fumed inwardly. Who did he think he was? God?

She had to bite her lip to keep the lid on her annoyance. Why didn't he just come out and say he didn't trust her, and the whole idea of her marrying into his illustrious family turned his stomach? she thought, defiantly returning his stare.

Most young wives, if they had any problems at all with their husbands' parents, seemed more often to be at loggerheads with the mother-in-law. Clearly, in her case, Salvatore was going to be the difficult one.

Hard-pressed to conceal the acid in her tone, she said, "In case you missed it the first time around, Signor Rainero, the whole purpose of our making a home for the children is to create as little disruption to their lives as possible. Relocating to San Francisco, or anywhere other than Rome, for that matter, would be counterproductive, don't you think?"

He inclined his head in regal assent, and the meal ended shortly after. And not a moment too soon, as far as Callie was concerned. She'd had about as much of Salvatore's overbearing attitude as she could take for one day, and when Lidia asked if she'd like to help get the children settled for the night, she leaped at the chance.

Perching on Clemente's bed, with him leaning affectionately against her on one side, and Gina cuddled up next to her on the other, and watching the telltale expressions sweeping over their adorable little face as Lidia read, in English, another chapter from *Sarah Plain and Tall,* Callie knew a deep thankfulness for the changes that had come so unexpectedly into her life.

This was what she'd missed with her children—the small, everyday rituals they'd cherish the rest of their lives—and to be given the chance to take part in them at last was nothing short of a miracle.

"Sarah's like you, Zia Caroline," Gina decided, when Lidia finally closed the book.

Callie laughed. "You mean, plain and tall?"

"No," Gina said, shocked. "You're pretty. You look a lot like Mommy. But you've come to look after us because she can't anymore, and that's what Sarah did in the story, as well."

"Yes." Stabbed by one of those sudden pangs of loss that crept up on her so frequently, Callie dropped a kiss on her daughter's head. "And just like Sarah in the story, I'll never leave you."

Clemente tugged on her sleeve. "Or me?"

"Or you, sweetheart."

His father closed the library door, went directly to the antique carved butler table where coffee and liqueurs waited, and poured two glasses of grappa. "All right, there's no one here now but the two of us," he said, handing one glass to Paolo. "So tell me, my son, what's really behind this preposterous idea of marrying Caroline Leighton?"

"I already told you. I want to put the pieces of the twins' lives back together, the best way I know how."

His father curled his lip scornfully. "And we both know you don't need to marry that woman, to do it. Or, if you feel you must take a wife in order to provide a mother figure, that there are a dozen other women more suited—possibly a hundred!—who'd jump at the chance to take on the job."

"But none as dedicated as Caroline to your grandchildren's welfare. Even you can't deny that she loves Gina and Clemente." His gaze clashed with his father's. "I expect you to find that reason enough to give us your blessing, even if you disapprove of my choice."

For a long moment, their gazes remained locked in silent combat—two men used to getting their own way, Paolo thought grimly, the difference being that the elder had years more experience in winning.

This time, however, his father was the first to break eye contact. "At least you don't insult my intelligence by claiming to be in love with her," he growled.

To ward off the chill of evening, Paolo knelt and put a match to the fire laid in the marble hearth. "How I feel about Caroline is irrelevant to this discussion."

A clever, smooth answer, delivered with enough dispassion that even his own father couldn't detect the lie. But there was no deceiving himself. His feelings for Caroline had undergone a huge change. He'd been falling more in love with her every day, and hadn't hit bottom yet. Probably never would.

Strange how things work out sometimes, he thought, poking at a log. Who'd have expected that what began with a funeral, would end with a wedding? That mutual sorrow would provide the breeding ground for love? Certainly not he!

The day he'd met her in Paris, he'd viewed Caroline as his family's self-declared enemy, one he was prepared to defeat by any means available. He'd been fooled by her aloof reserve, her icy control, seeing both as symptoms of a woman too self-involved to be touched by anyone's tragedy but her own. There'd been nothing left of the sweet innocent he'd once seduced.

Or so he'd believed at the time. Little by little, though, her brittle facade had cracked, beginning as early as that same afternoon when the twins' nanny, Tullia, brought them back to his parents' apartment from the park. At the sight of them, Caroline, who'd been taking tea with his mother in the salon, jumped up so abruptly from her chair that her cup overturned in its saucer.

"Oh!" she'd whispered brokenly, flying across the room to where the children hovered in the doorway, and folding them in a fierce hug.

He'd heard a world of love in that single syllable; a lifetime of something that, if he hadn't known better, he'd have identified as a regret painful beyond bearing. The twins, though, still frozen with a grief too large for any child to comprehend, had remained unmoved, not caring about her enough either to reject or accept her.

"Can you not say ciao to your aunt?" he'd asked them, surprised and not a little chagrined at how sorry he felt for her.

"Ciao," they'd recited obediently, and tried to wriggle free.

After that, for him, it had been downhill all the way. The cracks in her composure had grown increasingly more noticeable, try as she might to hide them. At any other time, his mother would have noticed, and done her best to console their guest. But his mother was drowning in her own sorrow, and able to offer limited comfort at best.

As for his father, so deeply ingrained was his antipathy for her that, if Caroline had collapsed in a broken heap at his feet, he'd have stepped over her without a second glance, and sent for the maid to clean up the mess.

Paolo, though, grew more enamored by the hour, even if he'd been slow to realize it at the time. How else to explain why he couldn't keep his hands off her, or stay away from her at night, or bear not being within touching distance during the day?

Why else had he proposed to her?

Oh, he might fool everyone else with his altruistic motives, and yes, his niece and nephew had figured hugely in his decision, but no use fooling himself. He wanted Caroline *despite* all the practical reasons for marrying her, not because of them. He was hooked, plain and simple. And loving every minute of it!

Unable to keep the smile off his face, he dusted off his hands and picked up his glass again, aware that his father watched him closely.

"You say your feelings for Caroline are *irrelevant,* Paolo?" he said scornfully. "Then I say, either you're lying to me, or worse, you're lying to yourself."

"You're entitled to your opinion, Father."

His father responded with a derisive snort. "Opinion, nothing! Admit it, man: you're besotted with her! She's bewitched you with her smiles. Undone you with her tears. And that is why, for your protection and that of my grandchildren, I intend to have my team of lawyers draw up a watertight prenuptial agreement. That the wretched woman's all sweet compliance now is no guarantee she'll remain so in the future."

Stopping dead in his tracks, Paolo struggled to contain the surge of anger scalding his throat. When he at last trusted himself to speak, he did so with feral intent. "Listen well to what I'm about to say, Father, and take it to heart," he snarled, turning slowly to face him. "First, you will do no such thing. And second, you will never again refer to my future wife with such contempt. I will not tolerate a repeat of it, for any reason."

"Bravely spoken, Paolo," his father returned, "but I'm afraid you can't control my feelings anymore, it would seem, than you can control your own."

"But *you* can control your tongue. You can and will treat Caroline cordially and with civility. And if you defy me on this, then prepare to be deprived of the pleasure of *my* family's company."

His father sank back in his chair, his color hectic, his breathing labored. "You would not dare deny me access to my own grandchildren!"

"Try me," Paolo said, refusing to show his alarm at the symptoms his father presented.

"Let me remind you that I am the head of this household, Paolo," he blustered, fumbling beneath the lapel of his dinner jacket.

"As I will be head of mine. You'd do well to remember that."

His father's color receded, leaving his skin an unhealthy gray. "You accuse me of not showing proper esteem for your fiancée, yet dare to address me with such disrespect?"

"I honor you as my father, but I would be less than you expected of a son if I were to let you ride roughshod over my wife. What, after all, has Caroline done to offend you? Is it the fact that it took a tragedy of monumental proportions for her to make the effort to come to Italy? The belief that, if it weren't for her connection to our family by marriage, she wouldn't register on your social scale? Your perceived notion that she poses a threat to your grandchildren? Or is it that she has carved out a successful life for herself, without once having to appeal to you for help, and refuses to be cowed by your attempts to put her in her place?"

"She shows no regard for our family's rich ancestry," Salvatore sputtered. "No understanding of my grandchildren's fine heritage. She is too American in her outlook and demeanor."

Frustrated, for this was an old and tired argument brought out and dusted off whenever someone veered too far from revered tradition, Paolo tried one last line of reasoning. "You once said the same about Vanessa, Father, and later admitted you'd misjudged her."

"She was different. She showed regard for our way of doing things. She embraced our values and our customs."

"And Caroline will do the same. Why else would she have so readily agreed to live here? Please, Father, put your doubts aside. Our family has been sadly depleted in recent weeks, and there are precious few of us left to carry on the name. We need to stand together now, not engage in pointless disputes that can do nothing but tear us apart."

For a moment, his father glowered at the suggestion, clearly ready to stand toe to toe with him on the idea. Then, abruptly, he leaned his head against the high back of his chair and closed his eyes. "Perhaps you're right," he said grudgingly. "Perhaps we need to make the best of what we have left. For that reason, and for the sake of my grandchildren, I will try to overcome my misgivings and welcome Caroline, as I welcomed her sister before her."

"You're very good with the children, Caroline," Lidia remarked, as they made their way downstairs after tucking Clemente and Gina into their beds. "I hope they come to realize how fortunate they are that you're willing and able to step into Vanessa's shoes."

"I don't suppose I'll ever really fill them, Lidia, but I promise I'll do my very best."

"I know you will. But you're giving up so much—your home in America, your profession, your friends. It's a lot to ask, especially when you've worked so hard to build a successful career."

But architecture had never been more than a substitute for what she really wanted. She'd have given it up in a flash, if she'd been able to keep her babies.

"For the next few years, being a mother and a wife will be my career, and I have no regrets about that," she said. "Architecture will still be there, when I'm not needed on the homefront."

"Oh, you'll always be needed, my dear," Lidia said with a laugh. "Just because children grow up doesn't mean they don't still need their mothers." Pausing at the foot of the stairs, she rested her hand on the newel post and shot a tentative glance Callie's way. "Forgive me if I'm speaking out of turn, but have you and Paolo talked about having more children?"

"Not really. Why do you ask?"

"Because having another baby might help close old wounds."

What an odd thing to say, Callie thought. Yet Lidia was regarding her with such compassion that she couldn't take offense. But the remark was enough to bring to the forefront the burden of guilt forever lurking in the back of her mind, and it left her stomach tied in knots.

Everything she'd ever longed for, and thought she could never have—her children, Paolo, *true* peace of mind, *real* happiness—lay within her grasp. But losing her sister and brother-in-law was a terrible price to pay for such a gift, and she had all she could do right now to cope with that. Confession, she had decided, would have to wait.

Suddenly, though, she wanted to tell this kind and gentle grandmother the truth. Wanted to ask her advice on how best to break the news to Paolo. And desperately wanted to know that whenever she did confide in him, at least one other person would be there to lend support, if she needed it.

From the outset, she'd felt a universal connection with Lidia, the kind that existed only between women. Lidia was not one to judge another person harshly or unfairly. Also, she was a mother; she'd understand that nothing was straightforward or simple when it came to protecting one's children.

"Lidia," she began hesitantly, "is there some place we can talk without being disturbed?"

"My sitting room. We'll be quite alone there. The men are enjoying their brandy in the library and won't mind if we take a few minutes for ourselves, I'm sure."

She led the way toward the back of the villa, to a little room with a glassed-in solarium at one end. Furnished with white wicker and pastel prints, it was as pretty and welcoming as Lidia herself.

"Have a seat, dear," she said, closing the door and indicating a love seat upholstered with plump cushions, "and tell me what's on your mind. Is it to do with the wedding?"

Callie had often wondered how she'd ever broach the subject. Had been sure she'd never find the words. But in the end, there were few from which to choose. "No, it's about the twins…about when they were born, and why I've stayed away from them all these years. The thing is, Lidia, the day Vanessa and Ermanno got married—"

Astonishingly Lidia leaned forward and pressed a finger to Callie's lips. "Hush, Caroline! There's no need to explain, and no need at all to feel ashamed or guilty for something that happened so long ago. You were very young at the time, very inexperienced and, I daresay, very frightened."

Callie's jaw sagged in shock. "You *know?*"

"Yes, my dear. I saw you stumbling back here, the next morning, with your pretty dress in disarray, and guessed Paolo had kept you out all night. I was very disappointed in him, at the time. Very angry. But that's all in the past, *cara*—a long-forgotten mistake that doesn't matter at all, now that you and he have found each other again."

"I don't think you quite understand what I'm trying to tell you," Callie mumbled. "The fact is, Lidia—"

But even as she gathered her courage to finish what she'd started, a knock came at the door. A moment later, Paolo poked his head into the room.

"So this is where you're hiding," he said. "Am I interrupting something important?"

"Not at all," Lidia said, patting Callie's hand briskly. "We were just enjoying a little mother-daughter talk, but we're done now."

"Good, because I've got a nice fire going in the library, and the coffee's waiting. Also, Father seems a bit under the weather and—"

Lidia rose hurriedly from her seat. "Then I'll go to him at once. Are you coming, Caroline?"

Left with little other choice, Callie followed her. When she reached the door, Paolo folded her hand firmly in his and bathed her in a smile so intimate that she went hot all over.

Noticing, Lidia slowed down long enough to fix them both in a fond gaze and said softly, "Have I told you how happy I am that the two of you have come together as a couple like this? Knowing you're forging a future together, and giving my grandchildren the next best thing to the parents they've lost, gives me the strength to accept the tragedy that has struck our family."

"It's been hard for all of us, especially you, Momma," Paolo said, pushing open the library door, "but things are going to get better from now on."

"Not if I have to wait much longer for my coffee," Salvatore boomed, hauling himself out of his chair and coming to meet them. "Lidia, *mia bella,* I'm glad you're here. Something I ate at dinner gave me indigestion, but seeing your smiling face makes me feel much better."

He wasn't the easiest man to get along with, but his abiding love for his wife was genuine and unmistakable, and for that Callie had to admire him. She could only hope to inspire a fraction of the same devotion in Paolo.

The library, with its paneled bookshelves, rich wine-red damask draperies and blazing fire was warm and cosy. Insisting he was quite recovered, Salvatore accepted a cup of coffee and fell to discussing business with Paolo. Reassured, Lidia resumed quizzing Callie about the wedding.

Where did she want to be married—in Rome, in a church, or here on the island, with a makeshift chapel and the family priest? Would she invite friends from America? What about after the ceremony—a lunch, or a dinner reception? And a honeymoon—surely she wasn't going to deny herself and Paolo the chance to be alone together for a few days, when the children had their grandparents and a nanny to look after them?

"I suppose we do need to nail down some details," Callie said, after Lidia had taken her husband off to bed.

"Starting with an actual wedding date." Blowing out an exasperated breath, Paolo joined her on the velvet couch in front of the fire. "As you've probably gathered, my father tends to steamroll over anyone who disagrees with his idea of how things should be done. The sooner we're married and in a place of our own, the better."

"He is rather…opinionated."

"Very tactfully put, *tesoro!*" he replied, with a laugh. "What do you say we set the date for two weeks from Saturday? That should allow us enough time to meet all the legal formalities."

"I hadn't thought about those. Are they very complicated?"

"Only in that you're a U.S. citizen. You have your passport with you, of course, but if you also happened to bring your birth certificate—"

"I did. I always carry it with me."

"Then the only other requirements are for you to make a sworn declaration before the Consular Officer, at the U.S. Embassy in Rome, to the effect that you're legally free to marry me. You'll then have to do the same before an Italian official, and for this, you'll need four witnesses to verify your claim. My parents make two, so it's a matter of finding two more, which might entail bringing a couple of your friends over from America for a couple of days."

"Actually not," she said. "A friend of mine and her husband have rented a villa on the Amalfi coast for the winter. He's a writer, researching material for his next book."

"Do you know where they're staying?"

"No. But I can phone her mother in the morning, and find out."

"Excellent. If they'll help us, I'll arrange for them to be flown to Rome as soon as possible. Once we have those notarized documents, we can then obtain a license in four days, instead of having to wait the usual three weeks."

"We're not leaving ourselves much time, considering everything else that has to be done," she murmured, settling contentedly into the curve of his arm.

"I agree." He stroked her hair. "So now that everything's out in the open, I suggest we return to Rome tomorrow, begin making the necessary applications, and start looking for a place to live. And once there, you'll find it much easier to finalize the wedding arrangements, and shop for whatever you need."

"What about the children? Will we leave them here?"

"No. It's time they were back at school. Time we all picked up the threads of our lives and moved forward."

"Your parents, too?"

"Especially my parents. My father needs to busy himself with something other than interfering with our plans. And my mother…" He glanced at Callie from beneath lowered lashes that were much too long and lush to be wasted on a man. "I know she's not your mother, Caroline, but if you were serious about letting her help you with the wedding, it would mean the world to her."

"She already knows I'm absolutely depending on her to help. She's a lovely woman, Paolo, inside and out. Don't ever worry that I'll resent her."

"You won't mind calling her Suocera?"

"I'd call her Mother, if she'd let me!"

"I'm sure she'll be thrilled. She misses Vanessa as much as she misses Ermanno. She and your sister were extremely close."

He tightened his hold, pulling her more firmly to his body. "We're going to make this work, Caroline," he promised, his mouth hovering over hers. "We're going to make something good out of this tragedy that has brought so much sorrow to our family."

When he held her like that, and looked at her as if she were the only woman in the world for him, she'd have believed him if he said he could turn granite into gold. What had begun as a teenage infatuation based on sex, had evolved into something deeper and much more enduring.

In the space of a few weeks, he'd established himself not

just as the love of her life, but as her lodestar. Nothing was impossible, as long as she had him at her side.

Reaching up, she traced her fingertips over the planes of his face, memorizing each feature. The dark sweep of his eyebrows, the carved cheekbones, the strong jaw. And the mouth that could flatten with displeasure, soften with amusement, or, as it did right now, curve with sensuous promise.

"We should make an early start tomorrow, and you're looking very sleepy, Signorina Leighton," he murmured, his lips brushing hers. "As your fiancé who is most concerned that you not appear as a bride hollow-eyed with exhaustion, I consider it my duty to take you to bed."

"I think that's a very good idea," she said.

They left for Rome the next morning, traveling by motor launch the short distance to the mainland, then the remaining two hundred and fifty miles in the private jet.

"Will you stay with us, Caroline?" Lidia asked, as they began their descent to Rome. "You'd have your own suite of rooms and all the privacy you want."

"Thank you, but I think it'll be more convenient for everyone if I book into a hotel," she replied, having already discussed the subject with Paolo, the night before.

"You'll stay with me in my apartment then," Paolo had said, when she'd expressed the fact that being under Salvatore's suspicious eye, twenty-four hours a day for most of the next two weeks, didn't exactly have her bursting into joyful song.

But tempting though it was, she'd declined Paolo's offer, too. "Bite your tongue!" she'd scolded. "Your father has enough reservations about me as it is, without my compounding the situation by openly cohabiting with his son and heir outside the bonds of matrimony."

Paolo had conceded her point, albeit reluctantly. "Then

since I plan to spend every night with you anyway, I'll reserve a room for you at a hotel conveniently close to my place. We're both consenting adults, Caroline, and what we do behind closed doors is nobody else's business."

"Caroline's right, Momma," he told his mother now. "We're going to be on the run, taking care of the hundred odd things needing to done before the wedding. It makes more sense for her to come and go without having to disturb you."

"But you'll still be seeing plenty of me, Lidia. I'm counting on you to help me with the wedding itself," Callie was quick to add.

"You already know I'll be only too happy to do whatever I can. Have you decided yet where you'd like to be married?"

Paolo shrugged. "A hotel, probably."

Seeing the disappointment his mother couldn't quite hide, Callie said, "If it's at all the same to you, Paolo, I think I'd like to be married at your parents' home here, in Rome."

His eyebrows shot up in surprise. "You would?"

"Well, it's quite lovely, and certainly big enough for what we have in mind. I think we could have a beautiful wedding there." She glanced at his parents. "If it's okay with you, of course."

"My family is always welcome in my home," Salvatore declared magnanimously. "We'd be honored to host your wedding."

Lidia, though, fairly squealed with unabashed delight. "Oh, Caroline, we'd *love* it! You must come over as soon as possible, and tell me how you'd like to have things done. The salon can easily accommodate at least forty guests, and if the weather is good, as it often is at this time of year, we can open the doors to the roof garden—perhaps even have the ceremony out there. Let me know where you're staying, so that I can keep in touch."

"I'm booking her into the Hassler," Paolo said.

"Perfect!" Lidia nodded, pleased. "You'll love it there, Caroline, my dear. It's right in the heart of the city, at the top of the Spanish Steps."

They landed shortly after, and scarcely had the jet rolled to a stop on the tarmac than the race against time began.

CHAPTER NINE

"WHAT do you think?" Twirling on the boutique's small, carpeted dais for Lidia's inspection, Callie showed off the last of three possible choices for her wedding dress, an exquisite creation of ivory silk chiffon cascading in a froth of creamy ruffles from the waist to the hem.

"They're all lovely," Lidia sighed. "I couldn't begin to choose just one. If it were up to me, I'd take all three."

"You're not helping!" Callie scolded with a laugh. "I really need some input here."

"I like the blue dress best," Gina said dreamily, clasping her hands beneath her dimpled chin. "You look beautiful in that, Zia Caroline. Just like a princess."

The designer, Serena, tipped her head to one side and inspected Callie as if she were a specimen under glass. "It's your wedding, signorina, and a day to be remembered. If you can't make up your mind about these three, why not choose the white gown you looked at earlier? It is classically elegant, and with a hat, or perhaps a wisp of veiling—"

"Oh, no hat or veil," Callie protested. "We're having a very small, simple wedding."

Serena exchanged smiling glances with Lidia. "There is no such thing. Small, yes, but simple? Never! In any case, you dress not for the guests, but for your groom. For him, you must have what you'd call in America 'a show stopper,' so that when you're grandparents yourselves, he will look at you and see not a woman in her sixties, perhaps with graying hair and a waist not quite so narrow, but his beautiful bride from years before."

Would he ever see her in such a romantic light? Callie wondered, examining the gown from all angles in the floor-to-ceiling curved mirror to the rear of the dais. Or would she forever be the other half of an equation arrived at for the children's sakes—because, although he acted as if he loved her, and although he called her darling and sweetheart, he'd never actually come straight out and said *I love you.*

But then, neither had she. In truth, she couldn't, not yet. She was afraid it would seem too much as if she was trying to soften him up and buy his forgiveness, if she bared her heart before she bared her conscience.

She'd hoped to have done that by now, but somehow the right opportunity never presented itself. The days were too full of other things, other people, and the nights…oh, how could she spoil the sweet intimacy of lying naked in his arms? How survive the agony, if he pushed her away and left her to sleep alone, too angry and disappointed to stand the sight of her?

The gown ebbed over her toes in a flurry of tiny waves. No question about its being the most spectacular of the three finalists, but although she wasn't normally superstitious, it suddenly crossed her mind that she'd worn silk chiffon at Vanessa's wedding, and it hadn't turned out to be a lucky choice. Paolo had tired of her within hours. She wasn't about to risk the same thing happening again on her own wedding day. She had enough to contend with, without tempting fate unnecessarily.

Mirroring her thoughts, though for different reasons, the designer said, "Signora Rainero is quite right, of course. All three outfits beg to be worn by a woman of your slender shape, but with your blond hair and blue eyes, the burgundy velvet makes the most dramatic statement."

Callie shot a smile at her daughter, who perched on the edge of her little gilt chair, clearly enthralled with the whole procedure of outfitting the bride. "For the opera or theater, perhaps, but for my wedding, I'm leaning more toward Gina's choice. I'd like to try the blue dress again."

The luscious, shimmery silk jersey slipped over her skin like cool cream, falling from a high empire waist to drape in graceful folds around her ankles. More lavender than blue, it changed from smoky-lilac to silver, depending on how the light caught her every movement. Tiny crystal beads adorned the bodice and short sleeves, with another band of beading at the hem.

Gina was right. Callie might not be a princess, but in that dress, she felt like one.

"Yes," she decided. This was the best choice. It felt right, it looked right, and it was the most elegantly beautiful thing she'd ever owned.

Serena immediately took charge. "An excellent decision, signorina! If you'll now decide on a pair of satin shoes from these in the display case over here, my assistant will adjust the gown's hem so that you don't trip over it as you come to meet your groom. Once that's taken care of, I'll send the shoes to be dyed to match your dress, and make sure everything's ready for delivery to your hotel by tomorrow afternoon."

"I know you're meeting Paolo for lunch and would like to shop for something for Gina to wear, before then," Lidia said, as they left the boutique and stepped out into the elegant Via Condotti, "but we have time enough to make another stop first, and my dear, you look as if you could use a rest."

"I am finding it all a bit overwhelming," Callie confessed. After the peace and quiet of *Isola di Gemma,* the frantic pace of Rome took some getting used to.

"Then a good cup of coffee is what you need, and I know just the place, no more than a five-minute walk from here. After that, I'll have my driver take us to *Bonpoint* which carries a wonderful line of children's clothing. I'm sure we'll find exactly the right thing there, for Gina."

A few minutes later, over cappuccino and almond biscotti, Callie said quietly, "Thank you, Lidia, for your help. I'd never have been able to do this without you. I wouldn't have the first idea where to shop, let alone how to get around the city."

"But you *do* have me, and not just to help you prepare for your wedding. Don't ever forget that I'm no more than a phone call away, *any* time you need me."

"Then let me ask you something now," Callie said tentatively. "When's the best time for a woman to reveal everything about her past to the man she plans to marry—before or after the wedding?"

Lidia pursed her lips thoughtfully. "I think it depends on the kind of secret. I'm not sure confession is necessarily good for either party. So let me answer you with a question of my own. Do you love my son, Caroline?"

"Yes," she said, hugely relieved at being able to admit at least *this* truth freely, even if it wasn't to Paolo himself. "With my whole heart."

"Then consider this. We all carry secrets, and some are best kept to ourselves, especially if sharing them brings nothing but pain and heartache."

But would it bring pain and heartache to Paolo to learn the children were his? Or would it destroy him?

Seeming to sense her quandary, Lidia went on, "What's past is past, *cara,* and nothing you do now is going to change it. For what it's worth, my advice is to concentrate on today, my dear, and on tomorrow. On the secure life you'll have with Paolo and the children. *They* are what matter now. You and Paolo have arrived at this marriage quickly. Everything is still very new between you. Perhaps when you're all more settled, then will be the time to share your most closely guarded secrets."

"What are you talking about, Nonna?" Gina piped up, a timely reminder that little pitchers had big ears.

Lidia exchanged a discreet glance with Callie, then took her napkin and mopped the creamy mustache from her granddaughter's upper lip. "About your being a good little girl and finishing your milkshake, so that we can shop for a pretty dress for you. Hurry now, darling, or we'll run out of time."

They found exactly what they were looking for at *Bonpoint,* one of Rome's most exclusive shops for children. A full-length silk taffeta dress shot through with blush-pink and palest lilac, and festooned around the waist and neck with tiny satin rosebuds.

By the time it was layered in tissue paper and put in a box, Callie realized she was running late for her lunch with Paolo, but, "My driver will take you," Lidia said, calmly ushering her to the Mercedes limousine waiting at the curb. "You won't keep Paolo waiting more than a few minutes—just long enough to be fashionably late, my dear."

Paolo saw her the minute the car drew up outside the restaurant and she stepped out, all flushed, breathless and beautiful.

"You weren't the only one shopping," he said, after she was settled across from him at his favorite table, and had taken a sip of the champagne he'd ordered. "But you are late, *cara mia,* which prompts me to think I should have bought you a watch, instead of this."

Her mouth fell open in delicious shock as he snapped open the sterling silver jeweler's box, and showed her the platinum ring nesting inside on a dark blue velvet dome. "Paolo!" she gasped, turning rosy all over again. "It's…it's…!"

"An engagement ring." He shrugged with deliberate nonchalance. "I thought it was about time you had one. Will it do?"

"Do?" She pressed a hand to her mouth and shook her head, apparently at a loss for words.

"It's a very good diamond, Caroline," he said, knowing she was more than pleased with his choice, but enjoying teasing her anyway. "Certified VS1."

"It's not a diamond, it's a pigeon's egg!"

"Three carats only. Not so very big."

She swallowed. "Compared to what, the Hope Diamond?"

"Not even close! The Hope Diamond is more than forty-five carats, and quite a different cut from this." He took the ring from its box. "Shall we see how it looks on your finger?"

It fit, as he knew it would. He'd "borrowed" a pearl dinner ring she sometimes wore, and taken it with him when he purchased the diamond, which accounted for the engagement ring sliding over her slender knuckle now as if it had at last come home. "How does it feel?"

"Perfect!" she breathed, turning her hand this way and that to admire the gem's fiery clarity. "As if it belongs on *my* finger, and no one else's."

"It does, *tesoro.*"

Just as you now officially belong to me and no other man!

"But much too extravagant for the occasion, Paolo."

"How so?"

"Well, we're not exactly...like other couples who get engaged."

Not in love, you mean? Speak for yourself, my darling! If I thought you were ready to hear it, I'd shout my love for you from the rooftops.

Shaken yet again by the depth of his feelings, by the vicious streak of possessive jealousy attacking him, he spoke more harshly than he intended. "Don't make an issue out of nothing, Caroline. It's a bauble, that's all. One I can well afford."

"But you don't have to buy me," she quavered, obviously crushed by his reply. "I'm coming into this marriage with my eyes wide-open. I know it's not for the usual reasons."

Remorseful, he lifted her hand and kissed it. "What I should have said is, one I can well afford, and which you well deserve. Admittedly ours might not be the most conventional marriage, but where is it written that only the ordinary deserves recognition?"

"I don't know," she said, the sheen of tears still in her eyes, but the beginnings of a smile touching her lips.

"There you have it, then. We're making up our own rules as we go along, and among them is the absolute necessity of your wearing my ring." He leaned across the table confidentially. "You *are* a very beautiful woman, you know, and Italian men are famous for finding beautiful women irresistible. I'm simply staking my claim before someone else beats me to it."

Her smile blossomed, became dazzling. "The world's also full of women who'd give their eyeteeth for a man as handsome as you, so here's another rule. If I wear a ring, then you must, too. A wedding ring, that is."

"Of course. Some traditions are worth preserving. Shall I order my jeweler to make a ring for me that will match the one I've commissioned him to design for you?"

"No," she said. "What you can do is give me this man's name, and I'll speak to him myself. Rule number three…you don't get to pay for your own ring."

Their lunch arrived just then, and the conversation drifted to other things. "Did you find a wedding dress?" he asked, over his tortelli and truffles.

"Eventually, yes. One for Gina to wear, too. And I believe your mother's shopping for an outfit, this afternoon."

"Then everything's running on schedule. Tomorrow your friends fly up from Amalfi, and we take care of the paperwork to get the marriage license. And this afternoon—"

She looked up from her langoustine salad. "We have plans for this afternoon?"

"Indeed yes! While you were busy buying clothes—"

"You were buying jewelry?"

"Among other things. I also checked out a few villas that sound interesting. I've earmarked a couple for you to see." He pushed aside his plate and took a quick glance at his watch. "If you're finished, we have just enough time for coffee, before we head to the first appointment."

"Is it far from here?"

"A little over half an hour's drive north of the city, at Manziana, which is close to where Ermanno and Vanessa lived."

She propped her chin on her fist, her expression troubled. "I've been thinking about that," she said. "Might it not be best if we lived in their house?"

"I believe, from something Ermanno once said, that under the terms of their will, it is to be sold and the proceeds held in trust for the children."

"I was wondering about *that,* as well. When do you expect the wills to be read?"

"Whenever it's convenient. Our lawyers have contacted us already, to set a date, but since there's no hurry on that, and you and I have so much else to do, I've put them off until after we're married."

"I'd have thought it might be better to get it over and done with now. Close the book on the old before starting out with the new, as it were."

"The children are the sole beneficiaries, Caroline, and from a legal standpoint must be present for the readings. But we both know that their parents' deaths are never far from their minds, and right now, they're excited about our wedding. Why spoil it with such a grim reminder of all they've lost?" He eyed her quizzically. "Did I overstep the mark by not discussing it with you, before I made such a decision?"

She shrugged. "Oh, it's not that, Paolo. But couldn't we be the ones to buy the house? It would surely be easier on the twins, to be back in their own home."

"Without their mother and father?" He shook his head. "Think about that, Caroline. We'd be imposing our expectations, our changes, on a household set to other rules: Is that fair to the children?"

"You make it sound as if we'll treat them like strangers!"

"More to the point is that we're the ones who, in a way, will be the strangers, trespassing on hallowed ground. I can hear the twins now: *Mommy didn't put my underwear in that drawer, Zia Caroline. You've moved Daddy's favorite picture from his desk, Zio Paolo.*"

She stirred her coffee thoughtfully. "I see your point. Maybe we are better off starting out in a place that holds no memories."

"Well, some memories will come with us, of course, and that's as it should be. But this will be *our* home, in which we'll do things *our* way, and establish *our* traditions."

"I suppose you're right."

"I'm always right!" he informed her, and laughed at the way her beautiful blue eyes widened.

"I can see we're going to have to learn to compromise," she said.

"I suppose we are. But you know, Caroline, our getting married is about more than just the children. It's about us starting a life together as husband and wife." He inspected her over the rim of his coffee cup. "Which brings me to another point. Ermanno and Vanessa chose a house big enough for four, and a couple of live-in staff. I hope, once the twins have made the adjustment to living with us and feel secure in their new home, that we'll add to our family."

Again, she turned all rosy and flustered. A charming picture, he decided. He'd have to make sure he caused it often. "I thought you didn't want to bring a baby into the mix?"

"Not right away, but—" He stopped abruptly, as a thought occurred. "Or are you trying to tell me you think our romp on the beach left you pregnant?"

"No," she said. "I know for a fact that I'm not."

"Then there's no problem. We wait until the time is right, yes?"

Another smile played around her mouth. "If you say so, signor."

"I say we get out of here, before I forget myself so far as to drag you under the table and make love to you," he replied, the desire she so easily stirred in him making itself felt. "That could take quite some time, and I want you to see these villas while it's still light outside."

Manziana, she discovered, lay close to Lake Bracciano, between rolling green hills. And the houses Paolo had selected? They were mansions! Palaces! Beyond anything she'd ever dreamed of occupying.

The first, Villa Santa Francesca, a rectangular stuccoed building surrounded by several acres of land, including an old English-style garden, had two floors, with the master suite on the main opening directly to the pool terrace. It also came with its own private chapel and small cemetery.

This last was what decided Caroline to choose the second. The children, she figured, hardly needed other people's grave sites as a constant reminder of what they'd lost.

Il Paradiso Villa sat directly on the shores of the lake, with sweeping views from the distant hills, to the dome of St. Peter's on the horizon. Gracious stone balusters marked the edge of the terrace, with wide steps leading down to a sandy beach. Fountains splashed in quiet corners, sometimes spilling from ancient carved gargoyles on the villa walls, sometimes from three-tiered stone basins set among the lawns and flower beds.

There were stables, with quarters attached for stable hands, and a swimming pool. A tennis court and a putting green. A coach-house converted to hold five cars, with accommodation above for a housekeeping couple.

The house itself boasted hardwood floors rubbed to a satin finish by the passage of many feet over the years. A huge wine cellar lay below a big, rustic kitchen equipped with the most modern appliances, as well as a massive, ancient stone fire-place. A pool table, left behind by the previous owners, stood in the middle of the games room. Seventeenth-century fres-coes adorned the ceiling in the entrance hall and main recep-tions rooms.

A carved winding staircase led to six bedrooms with at-tached bathrooms, as well as a nanny's suite. A smaller stair-case at the end of the upstairs hall accessed the third floor where, in addition to an attic that begged for the sound of chil-dren playing on rainy days, there were also two more rooms for live-in maids.

"What do you think?" Paolo, who'd left her to wander from one area to another without interruption or comment from him, joined her in the master suite after she'd ended her tour.

"It's incredible." She flung out her hands, encompassing everything from the stunning views outside, to the fine ar-chitectural proportions of the house itself. "This home was built with love and an eye for beauty."

"It's also undergone some major and much needed reno-vation. The plumbing is fairly new, also the electrical system."

"But it's lost nothing of its integrity in the process. Whoever undertook the upgrading did so with sensitivity to the original design. It's a masterpiece, Paolo! A gem of a house. It has a warmth I can't define that makes a person feel welcome, the minute she steps through the front door."

"Are you saying you can see yourself living here?"

"Oh, yes!" She closed her eyes in bliss. *"Yes!"*

"I was hoping that would be so." He snaked his arm around

her waist and pulled her back to lean against him. "It's my choice, too," he said, resting his chin on her head. "The agent's waiting downstairs. What do you say we make an offer on the place?"

She laughed and turned in his arms. "One too good to refuse?"

"Is there any other kind?" he murmured hoarsely, and covered her mouth with his in a kiss that stole her breath away.

An hour and two phone calls later, they drove back to the city with a signed contract in their possession.

And so the pieces fell into place, day after day, hour after hour, for the next week.

An early evening candlelight ceremony, they decided, under a marquee on the Raineros's roof terrace, followed by a cocktail reception. Throughout, a harpist to play selections from Purcell, Vivaldi, Beethoven, and Pachelbel. A four-day honeymoon in Venice afterward, during which time the children would stay with their grandparents.

Meetings with the caterer, the florist. Deciding on a menu, a color scheme. Choosing furniture for the new house. Writing thank-you notes for the gifts that started arriving within hours of the invitations being delivered by hand to a guest list which, somehow, swelled from a modest thirty to a mind-boggling sixty-five, sixty of whom Callie had never met.

Being photographed for an article in a society magazine. Taping a television interview—an event which brought home to Callie just how newsworthy the Raineros were. Good thing she'd followed Lidia's advice and splurged on several more designer outfits.

And during her free time? Shopping, shopping and more shopping! Finalizing the paperwork required by the authorities for a US citizen to marry in Italy. Dinner with Paolo's parents, during which time Salvatore alternated between genial and withdrawn, and occasionally looking as if just the sight of her at his table was enough to give him indigestion.

Haute couturiste Serena had been right, Callie realized dizzily. Her "simple" wedding had ballooned out of all proportion to what she'd originally expected.

The days were a mad scramble; a wild, exhilarating ride on a carousel running amok, with Paolo often too busy to keep her company. But the stolen nights she shared with him made up for it. Long, lovely hours made all the sweeter for the whispered plans, the murmured endearments, the quiet intimacy.

Then there were the children, the shadowed grief in their eyes lessening, their excitement at the new life awaiting them with their aunt and uncle most of the time driving away the ghosts of what they'd lost.

"I love you, Zia Caroline," Gina confided. "You remind me of Mommy."

"I'm glad we're coming to live with you and Zio Paolo," Clemente said solemnly. "It won't be exactly the same, but you'll sort of be our parents, won't you?"

It was all too good to be true, Callie thought, as the days wound down until there were only two left before she became Signora Paolo Rainero.

She was right.

It was. *Much* too good to be true.

CHAPTER TEN

EVERYTHING fell apart on the wedding eve.

Callie had agreed to spend her last night as a single woman with the Raineros, "because no bride should wake up alone in a hotel room on her wedding day," her future mother-in-law had decreed.

Consequently, Lidia had arrived at the hotel earlier in the afternoon, to help Callie pack her belongings into a set of new leather suitcases embossed with her married initials—all except for the wedding ensemble, of course, which was sheathed in layers of tissue paper inside a protective vinyl garment bag.

After one last sweep through the rooms to make sure nothing had been left behind, they'd summoned a bellboy who loaded everything into the Rainero limousine waiting outside the hotel's front entrance, and within minutes were being driven through the rush hour traffic to the apartment.

Paolo had been tied up all day at his office, making sure his responsibilities were covered by others during his honeymoon absence, but planned to join Callie and his parents for dinner that evening. He had not yet shown up when Callie and Lidia got there, shortly after five, but must have arrived some time between then and seven o'clock when, having laid out her lingerie for the next day and hung up her wedding gown, Callie showered and changed into a sleek black dinner dress, then made her way down the long hall to the library, for the customary predinner drinks.

The library door stood ajar, showing a fire leaping in the hearth, and Paolo and his father conversing quietly. Callie was about to announce herself when a fragment of the conversation between the men caught her attention.

"You believe this is the only way?" she heard Salvatore say.

"Without a doubt," Paolo replied. "My policy has always been, know your enemies and keep them close if you want to retain control. A man can't fight if he refuses to face facts, Father. He has to recognize what he's up against."

"What do you think she'll do, when she finds out?"

"She'll deal with the situation, because she doesn't have any other choice."

"What if she can't handle it?"

"She can. She will." He handed his father a glass: dry vermouth over ice, as usual, Callie noted peripherally, an uneasy chill prickling her skin. "You know better than to be deceived by appearances. Underneath that fragile exterior lies the heart of a lioness. I'd have thought you'd figured that out for yourself, by now."

"How can any man know what really goes on inside a woman's head?" Salvatore sank into his favorite chair and stared moodily into the flames. "Hell, half the time, I can't even see inside yours, and you're my own flesh and blood."

Smiling, Paolo leaned against the carved mantelpiece, his glass cradled in his hand. "Don't tell me you still think I made a mistake in asking Caroline to be my wife?"

"No. Your mistake lay in being in too much of a hurry. If you'd asked me before you proposed, I'd have recommended you think long and hard before taking such a step."

"Momma thinks it's the smartest move I've ever made."

Salvatore shrugged and drank deeply from his glass. "As I just said, I don't pretend to understand what makes a woman tick. But why waste my breath? You've made up your mind, and I'm not going to change it at this late date, so let's get back to what we were talking about a moment ago. I still think I should take care of business, and send for my lawyers. They could be here in minutes and have everything sewn up before dinner's announced—and read Ermanno and Vanessa's wills while they're at it."

"No." Paolo shook his head emphatically. "You do whatever you feel you must to give you peace of mind, but the wills wait until after the honeymoon. It's not as if they hold any surprises, after all. We both know what to expect. But I'm this close to getting what I've been hoping for—" he held up his hand and extended his forefinger and thumb a millimeter apart "—and I'm not about to risk tossing a spoiler in the works now, with my wedding day only hours away."

Suddenly weak at the knees, Callie stepped away from the door and sank onto a nearby chair.

What business was Salvatore referring to?

Why would reading Vanessa and Ermanno's wills act as a spoiler?

Why had Paolo lied to her when he said delaying the reading was best for the children, when his reasons clearly had nothing to do with them, but plenty, apparently, to do with her?

And most urgently, what the devil had he meant when he spoke of knowing his enemies and keeping them close?

The questions battered at her without mercy. And hot on their heels came the brutal answer, smashing her fragile happiness and laying bare the flimsy foundation on which it was all based. It had been staring her in the face from outset, as she'd have realized if only she'd kept her wits about her, and refused to allow sex to enter the picture.

Probably Paolo had known all along about her being the children's sole appointed guardian. Not so surprising really; Ermanno had likely mentioned it at some point over the years, never expecting it was something that would ever actually come to pass. Tragically it had, but by delaying the reading of the wills until after she became his wife, Paolo could pretend ignorance of the fact. What had he thought? That by marrying her first, setting up house with her, and drawing Clemente and Gina firmly into the picture, he'd render her powerless?

Oh, Paolo! she mourned silently. *Don't you know that you didn't have to go to such lengths to get your own way? I love those children far too much to throw their lives into chaos, just to gain the upper hand. There was no need to seduce me, to ensure my cooperation; no need to make me fall in love with you all over again. You could have had it all, without resorting to trickery and deceit.*

Crushed, she buried her face in her hands. This was what happened, when a woman forgot that history had a way of repeating itself. How did the old saying go? Kick me once, shame on you. Kick me twice, shame on me!

"Caroline?" His voice, filled with duplicitous concern, broke into her misery, close enough for his breath to drift warmly over the back of her neck. "What are you doing, sitting out here in the hall, *tesoro?* Are you not feeling well?"

"No," she mumbled, and bit the inside of her cheek to hold her tears in check. She would not cry in front of him. She would not let him see how much he had hurt her. "I'm feeling lousy. Sick to my stomach, thanks to you and your father."

"What in the world are you talking about?" he exclaimed, urging her to her feet and steering her into the library.

She had to hand it to him. He covered his tracks well, putting on an act of innocent confusion that would have fooled the most hardened cynic. "As if you don't know!" she said bitterly. "The next time you're plotting some underhand scheme, remember to close the door first, to prevent your victim from overhearing."

"Victim…overhearing…? I don't understand—"

"Obviously she was eavesdropping," Salvatore cut in. "Hardly an admirable character trait in a wife, if you ask me."

"I'm not asking you." Paolo aimed a repressive stare his father's way, before turning his full attention on Callie again. "I don't know what you think you overheard, *cara*—"

"Enough to know you've played me for a fool for the last time." Numb with pain and disappointment, she tugged the engagement ring from her finger and placed it carefully on the library table. "Since there isn't going to be a wedding, I won't be needing this any longer."

Incredulous, he said, "Don't be ridiculous! Of course there's going to be a wedding!"

"Oh, let her go, if that's what she wants!" his father snarled impatiently. "You don't need her, Paolo. You never did."

"In fact, he did and does," Callie snapped, fixing the imperious old coot in a withering stare. "But what neither of you appear to appreciate is that *I* don't need *him.*"

"I was under the impression that we needed each other," Paolo said stiffly. "When did all that change, Caroline?"

"About five minutes ago, when I discovered I'm merely the means to an end for you. Controlling the children's future is all that matters to you, and to do that, you have to go through me. It's just too bad I'm not willing to let you use me like that."

He closed his eyes in a slow, frustrated blink. "*Dio,* will you stop talking in riddles and speak plainly, woman? You're making absolutely no sense."

Woman? Affronted, she drawled, "My goodness, Paolo, whatever happened to *tesoro?*"

"Whatever happened to the Caroline I thought I knew?" he returned, a noticeable touch of frost coating his words.

"She put two and two together and came up with four. You somehow found out that I'm named sole guardian of Vanessa and Ermanno's children. That means I get to decide where and with whom they now live. *If* I so choose, I can take them back to the States with me, and there's nothing you can do to stop me. So how do you prevent that happening? By proposing a marriage you'd never have entertained if it weren't that you thought it was your only option."

She stopped just long enough to swallow the lump in her throat. "What really sickens me, though, Paolo, is that you didn't have to go to such extremes to get your own way. I admit, when I first came here, it was with the intention of exercising my legal rights, but I soon realized the only rights that counted were the children's. I was prepared to leave the twins here, with the people *they* love the most, and settle for being an aunt who loved *them* enough to put her own feelings aside and focus on theirs."

"Paolo...Caroline, what's going on?"

At the intervention of a fourth person, the three them swung round to find Lidia hovering in the doorway, her face mirroring the anxiety in her question. "Your raised voices carried so clearly upstairs, I was afraid the children might hear. Did I really understand you to say the wedding is being canceled?"

"That's right," Callie said. "It seems I've been living in a fool's paradise, Lidia. I've known from the beginning that ours was a marriage of convenience, but I had no idea until a few minutes ago that the man *I* was prepared to call my husband actually perceives *me* as his enemy."

Although Paolo didn't move a muscle, his bogus display of artless confusion froze into a stony displeasure that radiated from his entire body. "What the devil are you talking about, Caroline?"

"I'm quoting you, that's all."

"Then you've lost your mind," he declared flatly. "I have never once referred to you as my enemy.

"Oh, please!" She rolled her eyes in eloquent disgust. "My Italian might not be flawless, but it's more than adequate enough for me to have understood every word you exchanged with your father. Know your enemies, you said. A man has to know what he's up against."

"What makes you think I was referring to you?"

"Because of what else you said, particularly the part about your not losing everything you've worked so hard to achieve. Let's see, exactly how did you put it? Ah, yes!" She imitated his earlier gesture, holding her forefinger and thumb just as he had. "Something along the lines of 'reading the wills can wait. I'm not going to risk losing everything I've worked for, with my wedding day just hours away.'"

Lidia turned mystified eyes on her son. "You said *that,* Paolo?"

"That, and a lot more," Callie told her, the pain she'd so far managed to subdue threatening to rise up and devour her. "Including the fact that you think he's making the smartest move of his life. Silly me, Lidia, to have believed you were actually on my side."

"Caroline, darling…!" Lidia started toward her, arms outstretched.

But Callie shied away, so close to bursting into tears that she couldn't bear to be touched. "Don't, please! It's over."

"It is not over," Paolo snapped, his tone iron-hard, his face tight with anger. "But we will continue this discussion in private. You will not drag my mother into it—or my father, either. This is between you and me, Caroline, and no one else."

"There's nothing to discuss, Paolo. I've made up my mind."

"As I have made up mine," he informed her, taking a step closer. "We agreed to marry for the children's sakes, and regardless of what you think you know or don't know, I will not allow you to renege on that promise at this late date."

I will not allow…! There it was again, that autocratic Rainero trait rearing its ugly head with damning effect.

Standing her ground, even though part of her wanted to cower, she spat, "You don't have any choice. We're not living in the Middle Ages. You can't force me to marry you."

"No, I can't," he agreed stonily. "And if you really do suddenly find the idea to be so abhorrent, then of course I will bow out of your life graciously. You should know, however, that these 'legal rights' you speak of are not quite as straightforward as you seem to think."

"Don't try to intimidate me at this stage of the game, Paolo. I'll stand by my word not to take the children back home with me, but that doesn't mean I'm about to relinquish all say in their future. You'll be answerable to me for the decisions you make that affect them. Even in Italy, a will's a will."

His smile and his sudden lapse into his native tongue made her blood run cold. "*Precisamente,* Caroline, *mio amore!* And the wills drawn up by my brother and your sister, less than a year ago, assign guardianship equally between you and me, something to which, as co-executor with my father, I can attest with the utmost certainty. And since you've already agreed that the children belong here..." He spread his hands expressively.

She staggered as if he'd landed a blow to her midriff and knocked the wind out of her. "I don't believe you!"

"It's true, Caroline," Lidia said, and from her tone and the wounded sympathy she saw in the woman's eyes, Callie knew that it was.

"Now that you're fully in the picture," Paolo continued remorselessly, "you might wish to reconsider your position because, Caroline, as you must now realize, I don't *have* to marry you, at all. I proposed to you because I thought it would be the best thing for the children, for you, and yes, for me. I still believe that to be the case. But I must warn you that, if you elect to walk away, there is not a judge here in Italy, in the United States, or in Outer Mongolia for that matter, who will support your right to have *any* say in the children's future. You're hoist by your own petard, my dear. Either you decide to go through with this marriage, or you accept a very secondary role in your niece and nephew's lives."

His unflappable delivery of news that knocked out the very foundation on which she'd based her assumptions was devastating enough, but it was Salvatore's smug complacency that drove her to a terrible recklessness.

Without stopping to think about the consequences, she blurted out, "I think a judge might disagree with that, if he knew I'm really the twins' birth mother!"

For perhaps ten seconds, she had the satisfaction of knowing she'd put them all at a loss. The silence following her bombshell positively thundered. Then all hell broke loose.

"Good God!" Salvatore exploded, practically foaming at the mouth. "Is there no limit to the lengths you're prepared to go, to destroy this family?"

"It's true!" she sobbed wildly, the tears she'd so far held back flooding down her face in torrents. "I *am* their real mother!"

"It's a lie, something you've concocted out of desperation," he roared. "How dare you come into my house and pull such a stunt? And what's the matter with you, Paolo, that you stand there not saying a word? You have only to look at those children to see the family resemblance. They are Raineros to the core."

"Of course they are," Callie cried, beleaguered on all sides when even Lidia's expression turned faintly disapproving. "They look like their father!"

Salvatore grabbed the mantelpiece to steady himself. "You're saying you had an affair with your sister's husband?" he sputtered.

"No. I had a one-night stand with his brother who, in those days, thought nothing of seducing a virgin, and even less of protecting her against pregnancy!"

The fallout from this second bombshell, delivered too soon after the first, left Lidia so agitated that Callie was afraid she might collapse, and rendered Salvatore temporarily dumbstruck. He soon recovered however. "Your story is preposterous! Do you hear me? *Preposterous!*"

But Paolo stood as if he were encased in ice, a terrible emptiness in his eyes, a terrible deadness in his voice when at last he spoke. "So this is the secret you've been nursing all this time. I've known all along there was something. Just for the record, *cara mia,* what did you hope to gain, by waiting until now to make your dramatic announcement?"

With a futile attempt to control her tears, she said, "I tried to tell you sooner. The first night you came to my room, I started to tell you, but you wouldn't listen."

He inclined his head in mute agreement. "I remember something of the sort. Even so, if what you're saying is the truth—"

"It's not!" Salvatore exploded, thumping his fist on the mantelpiece. "Her story is full of holes. Think about it, Paolo! Why would she not have come to you, if she was carrying your children, instead of passing them off as her sister's? Why not give you the chance to do the right thing by her? And what did she hold over Ermanno's head, that he kept such a secret from his own brother?"

"Nothing! I did nothing!" Callie protested, fired by the injustice of his accusation. "There was no need. Ermanno was furious with Paolo. As disgusted with him as you are with me."

"Then why didn't my brother confront me?" Paolo demanded.

"He wanted to. He was prepared to force you to do the honorable thing and marry me."

"You'll be saying next that you talked him out of it!"

Restored by a blistering anger, she returned Salvatore's mocking glare. "As a matter of fact, Signor Rainero, that's exactly what I did. I had no wish to take a husband who had to be dragged to the altar with a shotgun in his back."

"A noble sentiment, my dear, but hardly credible," the old man said scornfully.

"Oh, it's credible enough," Paolo interjected. "Especially when you consider how being the mother of twins would have curtailed Caroline's lofty career ambitions. So she chose the easy way out, and gave away her babies. I suppose we should thank her for not having placed them with strangers."

"It was for that very reason that Vanessa and Ermanno begged to adopt them—one I resisted, at first, I might add. If I'd had my way, I'd have kept my babies. Giving them up was the hardest thing I've ever had to do."

"But Ermanno and Vanessa managed to persuade you anyway!" Salvatore crooned sarcastically. "Tell me, signorina, how much did they have to pay you?"

"That's enough, Father. Let her finish. I can hardly wait to hear the rest." Paolo's words cut through the atmosphere, sharp as a knife blade. "Do go on, Caroline. You agreed to their suggestion because...?"

"Because I was barely nineteen, alone, and too young to take on single parenthood with one baby, let alone two. Because Ermanno knew your father would be humiliated by the public disgrace his favorite son had brought on the family name, and your mother would have been crushed."

She drew a long, shaky breath. "But most of all, because you weren't fit to be a husband or a father. Even your brother, who loved you dearly, agreed you were nothing but a playboy, and that the last thing I needed was to find myself married to a man incapable of fidelity. So we did what was best for the children."

"And, coincidentally, what was best for you. You could pursue your dreams unencumbered by guilt or responsibility."

"Oh, I carried my share of guilt, Paolo, and more grief than you can begin to imagine. Because of one mistake, my entire life changed. No more going to Smith, not when I was sticking out a mile in front, advertising my condition for the whole world to see. No more carefree sharing an apartment with two friends from school. Instead I went sneaking off to university in California where no one knew me, and worked as a waitress to afford the rent on a basement room, where I lived until I went into labor."

Something crossed his face then, a fleeting expression of such bleak despair that it broke her heart. In that brief and telling moment, she realized the extent of the damage she'd done, and all she wanted was to run to him and kiss away the hurt she'd inflicted. But he spoke before she had the chance.

"You didn't have to be without money. Whatever else my shortcomings, I'd never have denied you a decent place to live."

But not a place in your life, Paolo! Not a place in your heart...!

"My pride had taken enough of a beating. I wasn't about to accept handouts from you, or anyone else." She spared Salvatore another scathing glance. "Not even from Vanessa and Ermanno, although they tried hard enough to help me out. But they'd done enough in offering to adopt my babies, and the money they gave me I put into a trust account for the children. They'll inherit quite a tidy sum when they turn eighteen."

Salvatore curled his lip. "A very touching story, I'm sure."

"And every word of it the truth."

"So you say."

"You'd like to see the trust fund statement?"

"No. I have seen something far more compelling. I have seen the children's birth certificates. Ermanno and Vanessa are plainly stated as the parents."

"Those certificates were issued after the adoption took place, as the law requires. But I have a copy of the official papers, which I had to sign in order to make the adoption legal.

If that's not enough to convince you, Signor Rainero, then by all means arrange for a DNA test at a laboratory of your choice, here in Rome, since you have such a low opinion of anything American."

"Gladly. I will see to it first thing in the morning."

But Paolo, who'd distanced himself to stand slumped before the fireplace with his back to the room, spoke over his shoulder. "It is not necessary. I accept the truth of what she says, and now I will deal with it—and with her."

He'd scarcely finished speaking when Gina and Clemente's high, excited voices carried down the stairs, followed a second later by the sound of their feet.

"My children do not need to witness this," he said, straightening his shoulders and turning back to face his parents. "Keep them occupied, please, and away from here until I am done."

"Of course." Lidia gestured to her husband. "Come, Salvatore. You don't belong in here, either."

For once, he didn't argue. Instead he let her lead him from the room and close the door.

Callie could hear her heart thundering in the silence they left behind. Paolo in his present frame of mind was a force to be reckoned with, and she had only herself to thank for that. "What do you mean, you'll deal with me?" she asked, fighting to control her mounting dread. "Exactly what do you have in mind, Paolo?"

CHAPTER ELEVEN

IF EMERGING the winner was what he wanted, Paolo knew he'd achieved it. Caroline stood before him, her lovely face drained of color, her big blue eyes glassy with shock, her beautiful mouth—that mouth able to lie so convincingly for so long—quivering helplessly.

But the only victory he'd ever wanted was to win her trust, with the hope that, in time, he'd win her love, too. That she was capable of the kind of monumental deception to which she'd just confessed showed how little he'd succeeded.

Even so, seeing how her body trembled, how she groped for the back of the chair in front of her to keep herself upright, melted the frozen core which, for the last several minutes, had held him paralyzed. Despite everything she'd done, part of him wanted to wrap her in his arms and comfort her. But the betrayal cut too deep. This was not a situation that could be resolved with a quick kiss-and-make-up.

Steeling himself to remain unmoved, he said, "Why don't you sit down? This could take a while."

"I can't imagine it'll take any time at all," she said, lowering herself into the chair as if every bone in her body hurt. "What's left to say? That you're disgusted by my actions? Furious? Save yourself the trouble, Paolo. How you feel about me is already written plainly enough on your face."

"This might come as a surprise, but you're not foremost in my thoughts right now. I'm more concerned about our children, Caroline—about how and when to tell them we're their parents, and what that news will do to them."

"Maybe they shouldn't be told." She gnawed wretchedly on the corner of her lower lip. "Maybe it's best to keep the secret and let them go on believing Vanessa and Ermanno are their parents."

"Even the most closely guarded secrets have a way of leaking out. Already, what until tonight was known only to you, your sister and my brother, is now shared by three more people. The chances of it one day accidentally being revealed to our son and daughter are significant. And even if they weren't, I'm not inclined to perpetuate a lie that never should have been told in the first place. They have a right to a truth that affects them so profoundly."

"Then when I tell them, I'll explain that it was my fault, that I'm the one who chose to withhold it."

"When you tell them? Oh, no, Caroline, that's not how it's going to be. We tell them together—all of it. How it came about that you placed them with your sister, and why."

"If we do that, they could end up hating both of us."

"That's a risk I'm prepared to take."

"No. You stand to lose too much. They adore you. You've been part of their lives from the start, whereas I—" She stopped as a sob shook her, and pressed a fist to her mouth. "I've yet to earn a truly secure place in their hearts. My betrayal won't inflict such lasting damage."

As it always had, her grief touched him too profoundly. She looked so fragile and alone, huddled in her chair; so *innocent!* Horrified to find his own throat thick with emotion, he looked away and reminded himself of the enormous deceit she'd practiced. There'd been nothing innocent about that.

"The day has yet to dawn that I'll hide behind a woman's

skirts," he said roughly. "I'm not proud of the way my children were conceived, but I'm very proud to be their father, and that's something I intend to make clear to them from the outset."

She sighed dispiritedly. "Then let's get it over with. One look at your mother's face, and they'll have guessed something's terribly wrong. It's not fair to leave them wondering if it's because of something they've done."

"My thoughts exactly. They can't be sent off to bed believing there's going to be a wedding tomorrow—not unless a miracle occurs and we somehow manage to salvage something worthwhile from this debacle."

She raised her tearstained face to his. "That's not going to happen, and we both know it. I've made too many mistakes."

"The most critical of which was in not trusting me enough."

"I wanted to tell you about the children, Paolo."

"I'm not talking just about that. Even as recently as tonight, you overheard me say something to my father which you didn't understand, but instead of showing faith in your future husband, you chose to think the worst of him."

"What you said sounded so…incriminating."

"We were discussing my father's health. Today, his cardiologist told him he's living on borrowed time and urgently needs open-heart surgery. He's afraid, not so much of the procedure itself, but of being left an invalid, and becoming a burden to my mother. These are the things you heard us speak of, Caroline…the 'enemies' which he'd prefer to ignore, but which must be faced and overcome."

Consternation, shame, embarrassment—the emotions ranged over her face, one after the other. "I'm truly sorry!" she whispered. "If I'd known, I'd never have confronted him the way I did. I'd have shown him more sympathy."

"He wouldn't thank you for it. For a smart man, my father can be incredibly obtuse at times. He seems to think not talking openly about his problem might lessen its seriousness. That's why he's yet to confide in my mother."

She massaged the bridge of her dainty little nose, as if to ward off a headache. "Then how do his lawyers fit into the picture? He was adamant that he wanted to consult with them as soon as possible."

"He has a horror of falling ill before the surgery can take place, and ending up in hospital on life support. To avoid such a possibility, he wants to draw up a living will." He shrugged. "As for dealing with Ermanno and Vanessa's wills at the same time, he feared from the start that you might try to take the children away from us, and believed that the sooner you found out you shared guardianship with me, the sooner your plans would be derailed."

"You didn't agree with him?"

"At first, perhaps. You were pretty clear about your intentions, and I admit I thought you posed something of a threat."

"But you didn't act on it. Why not?"

"Everyone was raw with grief. We needed to pull together for the children's sakes, not engage in a tug-of-war over who had control of their future. They'd suffered enough. Then, things changed. I came to see you not as an outsider bent on destroying a family, but a tenderhearted woman incapable of hurting those she loved. All at once, the idea of our joining forces in marriage made perfect sense—not for the usual reason, perhaps, but for very good reasons, nonetheless."

"None of which ruled out dealing with the wills."

"True. But we were on the island, the lawyers were here in the city, there were over two hundred miles separating us from them…" He shrugged. "Suddenly it no longer mattered who was named guardian. More important matters had come to the fore. There was a wedding to arrange, a new life to plan, a future to build. The children were excited again, looking forward, instead back. The wills could wait."

He grimaced, the pain of realizing just how much they'd lost, hitting hard. And all because, in their race to get married, they hadn't taken the time to build a foundation of trust. A sad case of good intentions gone wrong, and four lives thrown into upheaval because of it.

"Nevertheless, if you'd told me about the change—about us sharing guardianship, things might never have come to this," she said.

"Are you suggesting learning that would have prompted you to tell me the truth about the twins' birth? Because if so, I'm not buying it, Caroline. You had plenty of opportunity to come clean." He swiped a hand down his face, weary of the whole pointless back-and-forth. "*Porca miseria,* what does it matter? The damage is done, and bickering about who's at fault solves nothing, and merely delays what we have to do next."

"Speak to the children, you mean?"

"Yes. I'll get them. While I'm gone, give some thought to how you want to handle this, because there's no quick and easy way to pass along the kind of news they're about to hear."

They were absorbed in a game of Chinese Checkers with his parents when he found them. Unnoticed, he lingered in the shadow of the arch leading to the day salon, and looked at them as if seeing them for the first time.

His children…his son and daughter! Wonder and dismay swept over him in equal parts. How could have held them in his arms as babies, and not recognized them as his? How have looked into their eyes and not seen the truth?

"Zio Paolo!" Gina glanced up and caught sight of him. "What have you and Zia Caroline been doing all this…?"

His face must have given away too much. Her question dwindled into silence. Her smile wavered. Her little face closed. Tragedy had sharpened her intuition to a fine edge.

Without his saying a word, she flinched as if to ward off another unkind stroke of fate, and sidled nearer to her brother.

For Paolo to pretend everything was the same as it had been an hour ago would have been cruel. "I'd like both of you to come with me," he said soberly. "Caroline and I have something to tell you."

Without a word they left their game, clutched each other's hands and followed him down the hall to the library.

Caroline stood next to the hearth, twisting a sodden handkerchief in her fingers. A lamp on the mantelpiece shed a halo around her head, highlighting the pale gold of her hair, but leaving her face in shadow. Even so, the twins saw at once that she'd been crying and, as children usually did when confronted by an adult's tears, clung even tighter to each other and hung back, more apprehensive than ever.

"Did somebody else die?" Clemente ventured in a whisper.

"No," Paolo hastened to reassure him. "We do have news that's going to come as a shock, but it's nothing quite that bad."

"Well, whatever it is, it's making Zia Caroline look sad. Did you have an argument?"

Paolo glanced at Caroline. A tear rolled down her face. Unable to speak, she left him to answer, but now that the moment was upon him, he, too, struggled to find the right words. "We've…decided to postpone the wedding," he began. "We won't be getting married tomorrow, after all."

"But you have to!" Gina wailed. "You said you would! You said we were all going to live together, and you always keep your promises!"

Her outburst prompted Caroline to jump in. "Don't blame Zio Paolo. It's my fault everything's changed."

"Why is it your fault?" Clemente asked. "What did you do, Zia Caroline?"

"I kept a secret from your uncle, and from both of you," she said tremulously. "A secret I should have told you about, a long time ago. I shared it with Zio Paolo just a little while ago, and now I want to share it with you. The thing is…"

She closed her eyes and inhaled a long, deep breath, the kind a person might take before a death-defying leap from a very high cliff into a raging river. "Oh, my darlings, I wish there was a kinder way to tell you this, but I'm afraid there's no way to soften the blow of what you're about to hear."

"So just say it in ordinary words," Clemente said, fixing her in an unwavering stare. "Just tell the truth. That's what you're supposed to do, when you get in trouble."

Gina inched closer. "Have you decided you don't love us enough to live with us?"

"Oh heavens, *no!* I couldn't love you more if you were my own children, because, you see…you really *are* my children…and I'm your m…mother."

Astounded, Clemente said, "How can you be our mother? You're our aunt."

Caroline clapped a hand to her mouth and looked helplessly at Paolo, her eyes telegraphing her dismay. *Help me!*

Pretty choked up himself, he felt no better able to answer his son's question than she was. He saw the confusion her news had created in his children, and wished he could offer an explanation that wouldn't rock their world. If ever there was a time to whitewash the truth, it had to be now. But he couldn't do it. He wouldn't.

"You're silly," Gina informed Caroline bluntly. "You aren't our mommy. Our mommy's dead."

"Yes, she is," Caroline said, her voice drenched in tears. "And you're right. She was your mommy in all the ways that really mattered. But there's more you need to know."

Gina stuck her fingers in her ears. "I'm not going to listen to you, Zia Caroline! You're saying bad things."

"Gina, sweetheart! I know this is hard for you to understand, but—!"

"La-la-la..." Gina caroled. "I can't hear you! *La-la-la-la!*"

Clemente nudged her in the ribs. "Shut up, Gina! We have to listen."

She glared at him mulishly. "You can, if you want to, but I'm not going to."

"I'm afraid you both need to hear this, my angels." Caroline appealed to them both with outstretched hands. "Won't you please let me try to explain?"

Torn, they looked to Paolo for guidance. He nodded encouragement, and kept his distance. For now, at least, he'd let Caroline handle things her way.

Taking a seat in the middle of the sofa, she patted the space on either side in invitation for the twins to join her. They approached warily, and perched on the edge of the cushions like two frightened little birds ready to take flight at the first sign of danger.

"You must be very confused," she began, "and I'm sure you'll have many questions, once you hear the story I'm about to tell you. I just want to begin by saying there's nothing you can't ask me, and I promise to answer you as truthfully as I know how."

She stopped then, as if she wasn't sure how to launch into the details, but Clemente, never one to be easily sidetracked, gave her the opening she needed. "I want to know why you said you're our mother, when you're not."

"But I am," she said. "I know I wasn't here to look after you, the way other mothers look after their children, but I gave birth to you. Do you know what I mean by that?"

"Yes." Gina regarded her sourly. "Once, when Nonno took us to see some people who live on a farm in the country, a pig started having her babies. She pushed them out of her bottom."

The look of sheer horror on Caroline's face was such that, despite the gravity of the moment, Paolo had to hide a smile. *Well, you asked for it,* he thought. *Now deal with it, my dear!*

"Yes...well..." Regrouping, she took a breath and continued. "I didn't have a daddy to help me, and I was very young, only just nineteen—"

"That's old," Gina said flatly.

"I suppose, when you're only eight, it is, but I wasn't quite old enough to look after two babies by myself."

Looking more suspicious by the second, Clemente said, "So what did you do, sell us?"

"No, darling. There wasn't enough money in the world for that. Instead I gave you to my sister, because she had a husband who could be your daddy, and a house where you could live, and because she loved me so much that I knew she'd love my babies, as well. But it made me very sad to say goodbye to you. I wished so much that I could keep you." Her lower lip quivered. "I missed you every day, and cried for you every night."

"Why didn't you have a daddy for us? Did he die, as well?"

Her glance met Paolo's, then flickered away. "No. I just didn't tell him I had you."

"Why not?" Clemente persisted.

Like a deer caught in the headlights, she raised her eyes to Paolo again. "At the time, I didn't think he'd want to know."

"Does he know now?"

Again, that hunted, helpless look crossed her face. "Yes. And he's very angry with me for causing so much trouble in the family."

"I'm angry, too!" Gina, always the more volatile of the two children, jumped up from the sofa. "I don't care if you borned me. You're still not my real mother and I don't care if you don't marry Zio Paolo, because I hate you! And if you try to make me come to America with you, I'll run away!" She charged across the room and flung herself at Paolo. "I'm staying here with Zio and Nonna and Nonno. *They're* my real family, not you!"

"Gina," he said, gently unwinding her from his leg, "don't you want to know who your father is?"

She looked up at him, her big brown eyes stormy. "I already know! It's my daddy."

"Your *other* father," he amended, crouching down to her level. "The one who'd very much like to introduce himself to you and your brother."

Clemente inched across the library to join them. "Do you know where he is, Zio?"

"Yes." His eyes stung embarrassingly and he had to swallow twice before he could go on. "He's right here in this room, and he loves you very much."

For a moment or two, his children stared at him blankly. Then, as the impact of his words sank home, their expressions underwent a change, from uncomprehending to amazed; from fearful to relieved.

"You?" Clemente exclaimed in hushed tones.

"Mmm-hmm. Afraid so."

Gina speared him with a scathing glare. "You made us with *her?*"

"Hey," he said, stroking his knuckles up her soft, sweet cheek. "Whether or not you like it, Caroline is your birth mother, and as your birth father, I won't let you be rude to her. Whether or not you're ready to accept it, nothing changes the fact that she gave you the best parents in the world when she let your mommy and daddy have you."

"I suppose." Gina chanced another look Caroline's way. "If you don't marry my uncle, will you go back to America?"

"Probably," Caroline said. "Unless—"

Gina grabbed hold of his leg more tightly. "Promise you won't make us go with her! *Promise,* Zio Paolo!"

"That'll never happen, unless you want it to," he assured her. "We'll have to work out something else."

* * *

Something else?

Alone in the library, with no stomach for dinner or company, Caroline stared into the fire. Her children had left the room without so much as a single glance her way. She'd heard their voices, low and tearful, fading down the hall as Paolo took them to the dining room. And even though they'd given her no reason to think they might, she'd waited on tenterhooks, praying that before they went to bed, they'd come back to say good night. Now, with the clock approaching ten, hope had died and she was left with the realization that she'd lost everything that mattered the most to her: her fiancé, her children, her future. She didn't even have a place to hide, she thought, exhaustion seeping into her bones, because the mere idea of spending the night in the room awaiting her, with her honeymoon trousseau neatly stowed in suitcases she'd never use, and the wedding dress she'd never wear hanging in the old-fashioned wardrobe…well, it was unthinkable.

A log shifted in the fireplace, sending new flames shooting up the chimney. Something on the corner of the library table caught their reflection. Her engagement ring, she realized, left where she'd placed it.

"Discarded just like me," she whimpered, heaving herself to her feet to retrieve it, and cringed at the whining self-pity she heard in her voice.

If her life had come crashing down around her ears, she had only herself to blame. She'd known from the outset why Paolo had asked her to marry him. Even if sex *had* entered the picture in grand fashion, his proposal had had nothing to do with love, and everything to do with convenience. If only she'd kept that reality in the forefront of her mind, instead of drifting into the fantasy land of *what if?* the conversation she'd overheard wouldn't have had the power to derail her so completely.

She cupped the ring in the palm of her hand. It was perfect—the *only* perfect thing in her relationship with Paolo, and perhaps that should have been enough to warn her that it didn't belong on the finger of a woman capable of lying so unforgivably to the man she planned to marry.

At least she'd never confessed to her love for him. That was one secret she had managed to keep to herself, and thank God for it! She couldn't have endured Paolo's indifference to such a revelation, or worse, his pity.

Suddenly the door opened and Paolo appeared, carrying a tray. "You missed dinner," he remarked, his tone so devoid of emotion that it gave no clue to his mood, "so I brought you something to eat."

"Thank you, but I'm not hungry."

"Starving yourself isn't going to solve anything, Caroline." He advanced into the room and proffered the tray. "You can manage a roll and a little cheese and antipasti, I'm sure."

But just the sight of food left her queasy. "No," she said, turning her face away. "I really couldn't eat a thing."

"Something to drink then. We could both use a shot of something strong." He moved to the table and she heard the clink of the heavy crystal stopper as he removed it from the decanter of grappa waiting to be served with the after-dinner coffee. "Will you join me?"

"Why not?" She didn't much care for the stuff, but she'd have swallowed drain cleaner if it would dull the pain.

He poured an inch of the liquor into two glasses and joined her by the fire. "Are you up to talking?"

Listlessly she took the glass. "Is there anything left to say?"

"We can hardly leave things as they are, Caroline. Regardless of how we feel about each other right now, we have two children to consider."

"Have you been with them all this time?"

"Yes. It took a while for them to fall asleep."

She took a sip of the grappa and grimaced as it burned its

way down her throat. "I'm not surprised. They're miserable and upset, and who can blame them?"

He flung himself down in the chair opposite hers. "They don't know what to feel, how to react. Just when they thought they could count on their world coming together, it's fallen apart. Again."

"And all because of me."

He studied the liquid swirling in his glass. "I'd say we've both managed to make a royal mess of the situation."

"Probably because it was never about us in the first place."

"Oh, it was about us all right," he said flatly. "Let's not deny our relationship blossomed beyond anything we'd first anticipated. But somewhere along the way, we forgot the children were the primary reason we decided to marry, and as a result, we hurt the ones we supposedly were trying to protect. It's going to take a long time and a great deal of patience to rebuild their trust in the two people they should most be able to count on."

"Is that even possible, Paolo?"

"In all honesty, I'm no longer sure it is. But this much is certain—I will not have my children's lives subjected to any more upheavals. They've been traumatized enough, and it ends now. Tonight has changed everything."

Absently smoothing the ball of her thumb over the diamond she still held in her hand, she looked across at him, hollow with pain, and saw her own anguish mirrored in his eyes. "Whatever we might have had…it's gone, hasn't it?"

"Well, you tell me, Caroline," he said, bleakly. "Is there any reason I should argue the point? Do you see any way to pick up the pieces and put them together again?"

CHAPTER TWELVE

HOW DID the old saying go? *You can glue together a plate that's been broken, but the cracks will always show, and it will never be the same as it was before. Never again as strong or beautiful.*

"If I could wave a magic wand and make everything better, I would," she told him on a sigh. "I wish…oh, I wish for so many things, Paolo, but most of all, that I could turn back time and do things differently."

"I wish for the same, but it's too late for that. So I ask you again, can you see a way to pick up where we left off, and salvage what's left of the plans we made?"

Could she? The ramifications of his question tore at her.

Could she look at Clemente and Gina every day, and see her children, yet know that when they looked at her, they saw not their mother, but someone masquerading in the role?

I hate you…I hate you…!

Dear God, could she hear those words from her daughter again, and not die from the pain of it?

"Well, Caroline?"

"Have you discussed such a prospect with the children?"

"No. They don't deal well with uncertainty. And in the event that you and I manage to reconcile, I won't pretend they'll readily accept it. They're wary and resentful. In their eyes, you intruded on sacred ground when you laid bare the truth about Vanessa and Ermanno. Warming up to you again will take some doing, but it's happened once already, and it can happen again."

"I suspect earning their trust—and yours—is going to be the more difficult task."

"That, too."

Exactly! She'd loved him from the day she met him, but to tell him so now wouldn't ring true, because why wait until she had nothing left to lose before she risked all by baring her soul? No, the time for that kind of admission was when she could say the words without sounding desperate or needy. When she could be brave enough to say the words and not expect anything in return.

Desolate, she cupped her elbows and hugged herself against the chill that pervaded her despite the roaring fire. A bone-deep weariness had penetrated, dulling her mind, numbing her body. "I'm not sure I have the right to try," she said sadly. "In all honesty, Paolo, so much has happened tonight that I'm not sure about anything anymore."

After a pause during which his gaze seemed to pierce her to the very core, he said, with heart-wrenching regret, "I can see that you're not, and I won't press you anymore tonight because, to tell the truth, I don't have any answers, either. In an ideal world, we'd sweep aside our differences and go ahead with our plans, but too much damage has been done. We're all bruised and hurting, and healing isn't going to happen overnight."

"So where does that leave us?"

"I propose we step back from the situation and give ourselves some breathing room. Just because there's no returning to the way things were doesn't mean we can't learn from our mistakes and build something even better. But whether that's possible, only time will tell."

In other words, no promises, and only a very little hope. But at least he phrased it graciously enough to leave her with her dignity intact. She didn't have to grovel or beg.

He left his seat and came to stand over her. "You're worn-out, Caroline," he said, pulling her to her feet. "Go to bed and try to get some sleep. We'll both see things more clearly after a good night's rest."

"I can't sleep just yet. I'd rather sit here by the fire a while longer, and try to sort through my thoughts."

"Then I'll leave you to it and say *buona notte.*" He bent his head and dropped a kiss on her cheek. "We'll talk again in the morning."

Slumping back into her chair after he left, Callie felt the walls of the library close in on her in claustrophobic despair, and knew she had to get out of the house if she had any hope of restoring some kind of order to the chaos in her mind.

The children were asleep, and Paolo and his parents were talking quietly among themselves. She heard them as she crept past the salon door, Lidia sounding anxious, the men's deeper tones reassuring, but all their voices too low for her to distinguish the exact words.

Just as well they were so preoccupied. It gave her the chance to sneak into her bedroom for her purse, then let herself out of the apartment and walk as far as the square on the corner, where she hailed a taxi.

Forty minutes later, she let herself into the villa on Lake Bracciano, which she and Paolo had bought just days before, when the future had looked full of promise. The new draperies she'd ordered hadn't yet been installed, allowing the moon, rising full and bright over the lake, to shine through the windows. Not bothering to turn on lamps, she wandered from room to room.

Copper-bottomed pots hung from an iron bracket mounted on the beamed ceiling above the work island in the kitchen. The two refrigerators, already stocked with basics, hummed contentedly side by side. Brass fireplace tools glimmered on the wide stone hearth. Blue and white dinnerware lined the shelves of the glass-fronted upper cabinets.

In the dining room, twelve damask-covered chairs flanked the banquet-size rosewood table. "We'll use it when we entertain," Paolo had said, when she'd questioned the need for something so ostentatious, "but for everyday meals with the children, we'll eat in the breakfast room."

The same flawless attention to detail greeted her at every turn throughout the house. Elegant furniture, gleaming floors, sparkling bathroom fixtures, pristine linens, tasteful accessories.

Perfect on the outside, she thought miserably, but ultimately empty at its heart because the absolute sense of security and trust that turned a house into a home, was lacking. Had it been just she and Paolo, they could have gone ahead with their plans, willing to risk failure. Willing to make mistakes, to fight and make up, and hope that, in the end, they'd succeed in forging an unbreakable bond.

But they were not just a man and a woman drawn together by a powerful chemistry. They were parents, and as such did not have the right to stake their children's happiness on a game of romantic Russian roulette.

The only way they could ever stand before God and State, and exchange vows to love and honor one another until death did them part, was when they believed without a shadow of doubt that they could keep those promises.

That time was not now, and indeed might never come. And that, she realized sorrowfully, made her only choice clear. For now, at least, she had to love them all enough to let them go.

The decision made, she curled into a ball on the silk upholstered sofa in the formal drawing room, drained of all emotion. She didn't move again until first light.

* * *

He heard her key in the lock and met her in the foyer when she let herself into the apartment, just after seven the next morning.

"Where the devil have you been?" he seethed, so beside himself with anxiety that he was tempted to shake her until her teeth rattled, at the same time that he wanted nothing more than to hold her in his arms and never let her go. "Do you have any idea what kind of thoughts raced through my mind, when I discovered you'd left without a word to anyone?"

"I didn't think you'd notice," she said meekly. "I'm sorry if I worried you."

Stunned, he stared at her, noting for the first time how crumpled her clothing was. Her eyes were shadowed, empty of life, her face so pale, her skin was almost transparent. Approaching her cautiously, he said, "*Dio,* Caroline, where did you spend the night?"

"I went to Manziana, to the villa on the lake."

"*Our* villa?"

"Yours and your children's," she corrected him.

"They're your children, too, for God's sake! You're their mother."

"No." She shook her head. "I gave them life, but that's not enough to make me their mother."

He raked a frustrated hand through his hair. "What are you saying, Caroline? That you're walking out on them again, because you can't stand having to be second-best to your sister?"

"I'm walking *away*. There's a difference."

"Then please explain it to me."

"Although it kills me to leave them, at this point I think the best thing I can do for my children is to go back to the States."

"Caroline—!"

"Listen to me, Paolo. Right now, they need you and your parents far more than they need me. They need the security you've always brought to their lives—the routine of the familiar. They need to know that regardless of what happens down the line between you and me, *their* lives have regained the kind of stability they lost when Vanessa and Ermanno died. As things presently stand, I can't give them that, dearly though I'd like to."

And dearly though he'd have liked to argue the point, in his heart Paolo had to agree with her. First things first. The children took priority. "Why couldn't we both have shown such wisdom sooner?" he muttered.

"Well, better late than never," she said, showing far more acceptance than he was able to command. "So I take it you agree that I should go?"

"Would it make any difference if I said no?"

She smiled, a faded imitation of the kind of warm, open smile he was used to, and shook her head. "No."

"Then I agree. When do you plan to leave?"

"As soon as possible. Today, if it can be arranged."

"Well, go if you must, but know this—you and I are not finished."

"I hope not."

"We'll keep in touch."

"Yes, please! I want to know how the children are—how you are."

He touched her face, stroking his hand down her cheek and along her jaw. "Same here," he returned thickly.

She left that afternoon, and spent the long hours between Rome and San Francisco endlessly reliving the pain of her final good byes. Lidia's tears and hugs and murmured sympathy. Salvatore, so gray in the face, she'd been ashamed that she'd hadn't seen for herself that he was not a well man. The children, their gazes darting between her and Paolo, as if they feared they were to blame for things not working out.

"Are you really going back to America?" Gina asked, not

sounding quite as pleased about the idea as Callie thought she would.

"Yes." Aching to take her daughter in her arms and never let her go, Callie made do with a brief hug and knew the feel of her child's warm, sweet little body would forever remain imprinted on her heart. "It's time, sweetheart."

Clemente had tugged at her sleeve. "Does that mean we'll never see you again?"

She'd exchanged teary glances with Lidia. "Oh, no! I'll be back often to visit, and if ever you decide you want to come to see me, all you have to do is let me know the date and time, and I'll be waiting for you."

Gina pulled away, her lip quivering, her glare defiant. "Sometimes, you really make me want to cry, and don't you know you're not supposed to do that?"

"Yes," she said. "And that's why I'm leaving, because I don't want to make anyone cry anymore."

"We should get going now, if you don't want to miss your flight," Paolo murmured at her elbow, sensitive to the emotional storm about to burst. Over her objections, he'd insisted on driving her to the airport.

Misty-eyed, she hugged Lidia again, and pressed a last kiss on her children's foreheads. Then, half-blinded by tears, she turned to Salvatore. "Goodbye, Signor Rainero, and good luck with your surgery," she said, her voice shaking. "I really do wish you the very best."

He cleared his throat and half made a move toward her. "You don't have to leave because of me, Caroline."

"I'm not," she told him. "I'm leaving because of me."

Nor did it end there. She had to get through that last scene at the airport, with Paolo. "Don't come inside with me," she said, as he drew up in front of the international departure building, and practically fell out of his car in an effort to escape before she flung herself at him and sobbed all over his starched white shirt.

"Don't be ridiculous," he retorted, and tossed the keys to the nearest parking valet. "I'll come with you to collect your boarding pass, and walk you as far as the security gate."

The first-class ticket he'd reserved made short work of checking in, but saying goodbye…? There was no quick and easy way to do that, not when he stood there, his gaze searching her face, and hers devouring his. Not when his mouth lifted in the ghost of a smile and he reached out to tuck a wisp of hair behind her ear.

And oh, most especially not when his hand slid around the back of her head and he inched forward for a kiss that should have brushed fleetingly against her cheek, but instead landed on her lips and lingered there, excruciating in its sweetness.

"Remember what I said before, *tesoro.* This is not the end, it's merely a time-out," he murmured, his dark brown gaze scouring her face.

"I hope you're right," she said, making no attempt to stem the tears. "But I came from a broken home. I know what it's like to live with parents who put up with each other for the sake of their children. And it's not true what the so-called experts say. A bad marriage isn't better than no marriage at all. It taints everything it touches, especially the children. So unless we can both make the right kind of commitment to each other…"

"We can," he said. "It's just going to take time. Once the children have come to terms with everything—"

"You must board now if you wish to make your flight, *signorina,*" the attendant at the desk interrupted. "The pilot has been cleared for take-off and we're about to close the gate to the aircraft."

Callie nodded and turned to Paolo one last time. "See you,"

she said, the smile she almost managed dissolving into tearful misery.

"*Si,*" he replied, and when she went to walk away, reached for her one last time. "See you, too, my Caroline."

CHAPTER THIRTEEN

WE'LL keep in touch, Paolo had said, on that last afternoon in Rome, but apart from a brief email to acknowledge hers telling him she'd arrived home safely, she didn't hear from him again, and eventually stopped waiting for the phone to ring, or another message to arrive. Better to stay busy and pick up the threads of her old life, than yearn for a new one that might never come to pass.

So she flung herself into her work, staying at the office long after everyone else left, and sometimes bringing projects home with her. Then, almost a month after she left Italy, she was called to Minneapolis to supervise a hotel restoration.

She stayed a week, and arrived home too late on the Friday night to do anything but fall into bed, exhausted. The next morning, she awoke just after eight to the kind of warm, sunny early December day that made San Francisco the envy of so many other cities throughout North America. But for her, the sun never really shone anymore.

A day for catching up, she decided morosely, wrapping a towel around her wet hair after she stepped out of the shower, then slapping a mud pack over her face and throat, before wandering to the kitchen to scrounge up something to eat. Not that she was hungry, which was just as well, because nothing too appetizing awaited her. The refrigerator was empty, apart from half a loaf, the limp remains of a head of lettuce, and a block of cheese suspiciously green around the edges.

First on her to-do list, once she was dressed and fit to be seen in public? A trip to the supermarket, followed by a walk down to Fisherman's Wharf where one of the restaurants might possibly tempt her to eat lunch. Shopping in Union Square for a shower gift for a colleague's forthcoming wedding. Picking up a movie to watch that evening, when she curled up by herself on the couch, in front of the fire.

Oh, yes, and checking her mail and messages, just in case he'd been in touch. Any chore, no matter how small, to distract her from the gaping, aching hole in her heart that never seemed able to heal.

She'd plugged in the coffee maker and popped bread in the toaster, while waiting for the mask to work its magic, when the doorbell rang. Peeking from her living-room window, she could see nothing in the street immediately below her front entrance, although a black Lincoln was parked illegally at the curb, a few houses away.

The morning paper must have arrived, she concluded. She stopped delivery during her absence, and asked for it to be resumed today. Tightening the belt holding her terry cloth robe closed, she picked her way past her still-unpacked suitcase and downstairs to the foyer.

She slid back the lock, opened the front door just wide enough to reach out one arm and grab the paper, and almost fainted at the sight awaiting her. Two little faces peered back. Faces she hadn't thought to see again for a very long time, and even then, not wreathed in shy smiles.

"Gina...Clemente...?" she croaked, afraid she was caught up in a cruel dream.

"Hello, Zia Momma," they chorused, looking so mightily pleased with themselves that, for all that she was too shocked to think straight, she knew they'd rehearsed the greeting ahead of time. Then, taking a second look at her, they nudged each other in the ribs and subsided into a fit of giggles.

Fairly sagging against the door frame, she pressed a fist to her racing heart. "What in the world are you doing *here?*"

"Well, you said we could visit you whenever we wanted, so we did," Gina said, as if only an idiot would fail to see the logic of such a move. "Aren't you going to invite us in?"

She dragged the door wider and gestured weakly. "Of course. But how—who brought you?"

"I did," the deep, dark Mediterranean voice that had haunted her night and day for the last month, supplied. "May I come in, too?"

She recoiled in horror. *"Paolo?"*

"Well, I didn't expect you'd roll out the red carpet," he said, his trademark charming smile not quite as poised as usual, "but I hoped you'd be at least a little pleased to see me."

"I'm wearing a towel on my head!" she squeaked. "I've got a mud pack slathered all over my face! Why would I be pleased to see anyone, let alone *you,* looking the way I do?"

"You're beautiful in my eyes, Caroline," he said, following the children into her foyer and closing the door, "although you ought to know your cosmetic clay is cracking badly. Perhaps you shouldn't be talking until it's finished cooking, and satisfy yourself with just listening to us, instead."

"I wasn't expecting company!"

"You mean, you didn't get my message, telling you we'd be stopping by?" He shrugged philosophically. "Oh, well, too late now. We're already here. I'd kiss you hello, but this doesn't seem the most appropriate moment to do so. Close your mouth, darling. You're beginning to drool."

Thoroughly restored to his usual in-charge self again, he pushed her ahead of him up the stairs, and somehow she made it all the way without tripping over her feet, even though her pulse was racing so fast, it left her dizzy.

"Please make yourselves at home and excuse me a moment," she managed, showing her three guests into the living room, and promptly fled to her en suite bathroom.

Her children were here, and they were smiling at her!

Paolo had called her *"darling!"* He'd never called her *"darling"* before!

And, oh dear heaven, when she most needed to put on her best face, she looked like a reject from a bad Halloween party! Although she had no memory of doing so, she'd started to cry, and her tears had left soggy ravines in her blue mud pack.

Appalled, she splashed cold water over the offending mask, and wiped it away with a facecloth. Whipped off the towel and dragged a comb through her hair. At least it had enough natural bounce not to hang in rats' tails around her face.

No time for makeup, she decided, afraid if she took too long to get ready, Paolo might grow tired of waiting. A spritz of cologne would have to do. And clothes, of course—underwear, a pair of pale green linen slacks, and a cream cashmere sweater she'd bought at Nordstrom's and never bothered to wear, because she'd had no one to dress up for.

"I poured us both coffee," Paolo said, handing her a steaming mug when she returned to find him and the children in her kitchen. "Sit down, darling, before you fall down."

Darling, again!

"Thank you." She seized the mug gratefully. She needed fortifying. Badly! "I'm sorry I can't offer you cookies, or something, but my cupboards are rather bare right now," she told the children, aware they were watching her as if they thought she might suddenly sprout two heads. "If I'd known you were coming, I'd have stocked up—"

"I'll take us all out for breakfast later," Paolo said. "But we have business to discuss first. A proposition we'd like to put to you." He cocked an eyebrow at the twins. "Which one of you would like to begin?"

After a pause, Clemente cleared his throat. “I will.”

“Well, get on with it then,” Gina prompted, when he seemed unable to decide what to say next. “It’s really easy. Just ask her if she’ll come back home with us.”

Callie’s heart quite literally stopped. For the longest second in recorded history, she hung suspended between heaven and earth, unsure where she was going to end up.

“Will you?” her son finally asked, timidly. “We’ve talked about it a lot, and we really wish you’d say yes. We didn’t think we would, but we miss you. And now that we’ve had time to think about it some more, we don’t mind that you’re our mother. It’s really quite all right, in fact.”

“Except you’re only our Other Mother,” Gina put in. “You can’t take our real mommy’s place.”

“No,” Callie whispered, those damnable tears threatening again. “I know I never could, nor would I wish to. No one can ever replace your mommy. She was much too special, to all of us.” She chanced a look at Paolo, who leaned against the kitchen counter, his face impassive. “But as far as my coming to live with you—”

“You might as well,” her pragmatic little daughter piped up. “Zio Poppa says the house is way too big for just the three of us.”

“Poppa?” Surprised, she looked his way again.

He gave another shrug. “They’re coming around, Caroline. They’re ready to deal with the truth.”

“Is that why you brought them to me?”

“Not entirely. I have my own agenda, too.” He drained his mug and set it on the counter. “Is there someplace the kids can entertain themselves with something on television, so that you and I can have a little privacy?”

“There’s a set in the living room, and although I can’t swear to it from personal experience, my married friends tell me their children love Saturday morning cartoons.”

"Good enough." With a sweeping motion, he herded the children to the living room, and was back within minutes. Alone.

"Do you care for more coffee?" she asked, suddenly not sure she was ready to hear what he had to say.

"No," he said, closing in on her. "I don't need coffee, but I very much need to do this."

He kissed her, then. At length. With his whole heart. With tenderness and restrained passion and a promise of better things to come.

"Ah, Caroline," he murmured, when they both surfaced for air. "I've waited much too long to do that. And even longer to beg your forgiveness, and tell you that I cannot live without you."

Afraid to burst the bubble of hope taking shape all around her, she said, "The children are too much of a handful?"

"No, *tesoro.* The children are exactly what they're supposed to be. Impossible to predict, not always easy to please, and thoroughly adorable. But my being only half the equation they need leaves me too often at a loss."

Disappointment, cold and damp as a San Francisco fog, clouded the clear surface of that magical bubble. "If you're here because you can't manage them on your own, the solution's pretty straightforward. Hire a nanny."

"If that's all it would take to ease the ache in my heart, I would. But my problem runs much deeper. Learning to be a father occupies me well enough during the day, but the long, empty hours of the nights, Caroline, are when a man must look into his heart and accept the truth that's been lurking there for weeks."

"You need a woman."

"I need you."

"Because my being the children's birth mother makes me the best candidate for the job? We've gone that route once already, Paolo," she said, the disappointment swirling around her now so thick and black it almost choked her, "and look how it ended."

He dragged his fingers through his hair, more beside himself than she'd ever thought to see him. "Caroline, *mio amore,* I'm here to beg your forgiveness."

He had tears in his eyes, she realized. They sparkled like diamonds, touching her so deeply that her heart turned over.

Shame tinting his words, he went on, "I seduced you and cast you aside without a second thought, even knowing, as I did by then, that you were an innocent, no more able to match a man of my experience than the babies you eventually bore because of me."

"That doesn't excuse my keeping the pregnancy from you. I should have told you right away."

"What woman in her right mind would have risked her children's future by confiding in such a man as I was then? Yet when we met again, both devastated by grief, you welcomed me into your arms and your bed with the same sweet generosity which, if I'd not been too consumed with selfishness to recognize it, you'd given yourself to me, the first time."

Overcome, he stopped and turned away from her. "I'm making a fool of myself, and embarrassing both of us," he choked.

Daring to touch him, she laid a hand against his shoulder. It trembled at the contact. "Not if you're speaking from your heart, Paolo," she said softly. "There's no shame in that."

He drew in a great, shuddering breath. "I don't need you because of the children, or because I lie alone in bed every night, aching for you. I need you because I love you, Caroline."

The sun, shining patiently since dawn to little effect, bathed her in a flood of warm, golden light. *"Love me?"*

"Love you," he reiterated shakily. "More than you can begin to know."

"Are you sure?"

"You are my heart, my life," he said, turning back and catching her hands. "God forgive me, I've known it for weeks and been too proud to admit it. But saying goodbye to you at the airport, watching you walk away, really brought it home to me. Seeing you leave…it nearly killed me, Caroline."

"Why didn't you say something before now, then?" she cried, mourning all the wasted days, the pain-filled hours. "I'd given up hope of ever hearing from you again."

"There were difficulties to be ironed out, with the children, and I wanted them resolved before I came to you. We're a package deal, I know, *tesoro,* but you'd been through enough. I couldn't put you through more." He dropped to one knee before her, and pressed her hand between both of his. "But the worst is over and I'm here now, doing the right thing for all the right reasons, and begging you to give me another chance."

She longed to believe him. Wanted to grab the brass ring he was offering, and never let it go. But old heartache made her wary. "Does your father know you're here, and why?"

"My father is recovering from triple bypass surgery. But yes, he knows, and if it matters any, he's in much more mellow spirits now that his health is on the mend. He won't give you any more grief. As for my mother, she waits anxiously to hear that I'm bringing you home again. But after all is said and done, *mio amore,* it's what *you* want that counts."

He gazed up at her, his expression sober, his eyes speaking volumes of uncertainty. "You already know I'm far from perfect, and always will be. As you've no doubt discovered for yourself, my faults are legion. But I give you my most solemn word that, if you'll give me another chance, I'll spend the rest of my life making our marriage something so rare and beautiful that you'll never regret becoming my wife. One way or another, I will win your love."

What point in pretending, when her heart was bursting to speak a truth too long held in abeyance? The time was past for playing mind games.

"Oh, Paolo," she wept, the tears streaming down her face. "Don't you know it's already yours to keep, for however long we live? I've loved you for nine years. I couldn't stop now, even I tried."

His jaw dropped. "How *could* I have known, when you never said a word?"

"At first, I was afraid to tell you, in case I scared you off. When you proposed, you did make it clear that ours was to be a marriage of convenience, after all."

"Caroline, after all those nights we spent together, you surely knew the terms of the contract had changed!"

"I…dared to hope. Things *seemed* to be different. But when you never confirmed it, I thought it was just my imagination. Not only that, but to tell you how I felt, when I knew I was keeping the secret of the children's birth from you—well, that didn't seem right, either. Then the truth came out anyway, but in such a way that it ripped apart the fabric of your family's life. After that, I didn't think you'd want to hear me say, *I love you.* I thought I'd left it too late, and you wouldn't want me at any price."

In one swift move, he was on his feet and folding her in his arms. "Not a chance," he said huskily. "This is where you belong, next to my heart for the rest of time. Marry me, and I will never let you go again. Come home again, Caroline. Your children need you desperately, and so do I."

"He's telling the truth, Zia Momma," Clemente said, apparently finding Saturday morning cartoons on television not nearly as riveting as real-life romantic drama in the kitchen.

"Yes, he is," her daughter chipped in. "So you might as well say yes, because we got a puppy after you left, and he's lonely without us. We need to get back to him fast, before he chews another hole in the rug."

Disentangling herself from Paolo's hold, Callie stepped back far enough to rest her gaze on one beloved face after another.

Her children, so beautiful, so forgiving, that she wanted to fall down on her knees and thank God for the gift of them.

Paolo, so strong and sure, he made her believe in miracles. How could she not, when three of them stood around her, close enough to touch?

She took a breath. Held open her arms and felt her heart soar as her children raced into her embrace. "I love you," she whispered into their sweet-smelling hair. "I always have and I always will."

"So don't cry then," Gina sniffled. "We decided we love you as well, so let's just get on with it, then we can all go home. Don't you know it'll soon be Christmas, and we've been waiting for you to come back, before we put up a tree?"

She heard Paolo's stifled laughter, felt his hand at her waist. Looked up and saw the love in his eyes, and the hope. "Well, that won't do at all," she said. "It takes time to put up the perfect Christmas tree. Don't just stand there, Paolo. We're all starving. Take us to breakfast, then take us home, my love."

"I was hoping that would be your decision, *tesoro,* which is why I have the jet fueled up, breakfast already waiting on board and my pilot ready for take-off as soon as I give him the word. How long will it take you to pack?"

"No time at all," she said, leaning into him and loving the strong steady beat of his heart beneath her hand. "Everything I need is right here in this room."

HARLEQUIN®
Presents